CH00842290

Hostage At Pottery Cottage

A Novella by Catherine Wood

Although this book is very loosely based on real events and in a real place, the names of characters have been changed and the story has been wildly altered from anything that actually happened

Dedicated to;

My Father for giving me time, my Mother for giving me imagination, my Sister for giving me advice and my Brother for giving me a kick up the bum!

My Son Samuel whom I strive to make proud every day

And

My Mamma, Phyllis May Allen, who taught me how to string a yarn and is the best, yet most modest story teller in the whole world!

Thank you all!

BANG!

She jolted awake at the sound of the gunshot, the gunshot that she would never hear yet reverberated around in her mind whenever she was alone.

Isn't it strange that, after something terrible has happened, the things that could have been different are often the ones that stay with you the longest? The things you could have done to make it all better, the things that could have made it even worse and the things that you could have done to prevent it ever happening at all.

It doesn't matter that these things are irrelevant to an event that can never be changed, you focus on them all the more, and sometimes when something so huge has shook your world, the memory of the things that could have happened are the ones that stay with you as sharply and clearly as if you were back in the moment reliving what could have been, forever.

Susan Johnson had once been the proud owner of a pristine kitchen. In fact her whole lifestyle had been uncluttered and efficient almost to the point of sterility.

Her rule had always been "a place for everything and everything in its place", but not anymore.

It didn't seem to matter how often she cleaned or tidied, the other four people in the house soon undid all her hard work and cluttered everything up again. It was a never ending task, caring for the people she held dearest. After years of trying to keep them in line with her ideals she had pretty much given up trying to control everything and learned to be a little more relaxed.

Even though Susan wished her house looked like a show home, she knew she wouldn't really change a thing. Every muddy wellington print and torn jumper was a tiny memory made by the people that she loved the most. Her ever increasing ease with family life and the mayhem it brought with it shocked no one more than Susan herself.

She had been born in Sheffield, and though she loved the people and the town, she had somehow always felt out of place. Her father was a steel worker, as most men of his age in an area famed for its steel industry, and her mother had been a housewife.

Susan had spent her childhood looking at her parents and feeling that somehow they had wasted their lives. At a young age she decided that she wanted to do something extraordinary with hers and began to apply herself at school and work hard to get ahead academically. When she finished school and went to college, after which she took an apprenticeship at a small publishing firm, Arkwright's. She had spent years working up to be a manager in Arkwright's Publishing Firm, but somehow she still didn't feel quite as fulfilled as she had imagined, even when she gained further promotion to become a director of the company. Yet she carried on in the hope that she would find what she was looking for, that simple thing that would make her life extraordinary.

She had been very vain, with her naturally wavy hair tamed straight and constantly restrained by grips. Her makeup was always kept immaculate to cover her olive complexion and emphasize her big brown eyes. Even though she was fairly tall she wore heels at all times and a suit to show she meant business in a man's world. With the little spare time she had she exercised and had a sleek body that she knew made her suits look excellent. She even learned to shake off her Sheffield accent just because she thought it would make her less professional if she didn't, something she knew made her mother sad.

She had been a career woman to the core and she had been good at it too. With her minimalist flat in town and her cocktails with the girls, she loved the professional single life and she had gradually distanced herself from her parents, even though she loved them very much she felt only a kind of sympathy for their simple lives which made her visits to them hung with gloom.

She had tried to understand why they felt so contended with their lot in life but it made no sense. They had always had enough money to be comfortable, but they had never had the luxuries in life that Susan felt were important to be happy. On occasion they had to scrimp and save for something big. They had bought her a car for her seventeenth birthday and Susan knew that they had been forced to sacrifice to save for it. She knew she should have felt like this made the car special and bought for her with love, but it just made her feel guilty and sad.

They couldn't see why she felt so distant from them, and it made her father angry sometimes. He would insist that he was content with everything they had, and that saving for things made them more worthwhile, but Susan was blind to this. She always had a little extra money just in case and she always had enough back to put towards her sleek new car and her designer clothes.

Mark, in comparison to his wife, revelled in the disorder his family created. Not mess as such, but the creature comforts close to hand. He knew his wife saw it differently to him but he couldn't abide cold crisp lines and sterile cleanliness. It reminded him of the days before he met her and made his children, the days when he was alone, with no real possessions to make a mess with.

Mark was in the graphic design trade. He too had worked hard to create a business, make a name for his company and be successful. He was doing well for himself too.

Mark had never found it hard to succeed. He knew he wasn't especially clever, he had simply managed to scrape through school with the minimum he needed, but he had something that couldn't be taught. He was simply charismatic. He was a chancer and cheeky, and everyone loved him, without him needing to try and make them, and if they didn't he couldn't care less.

He had made his business a success by asking for favours that others would blush to think of and getting those favours granted because people found his nerve endearing and refreshing.

His looks too, added to his mischievously lovable persona. He was tall, and had always been a little gangly. He had tried going to the gym to gain some tone to his physique but was far too lanky to produce any real muscles and gave it up before he had even really begun. His hair, a mousy brown, was impossible to tame, despite being trimmed by the best barber in the town. His face, and he would admit this himself, wasn't especially handsome, not until he smiled. There was something about Mark's smile that changed his whole being. He was fairly none descript and could hide easily in a crowd, but his smile made people stop and listen. It was the sort of smile that was infections and when he flashed his pearly whites it was always offered a smile in return. This made it almost effortless for Mark to get ahead in business, he loved pitching new ideas to people and trying to get away with things that he knew he shouldn't.

He, like Susan, had a sparsely decorated white penthouse flat and enough money to buy pretty much anything he desired, though little time to enjoy it. Mark Johnson lived to work, but unlike Susan, he knew he was not contented by success alone, and never would be.

Regardless of their achievements neither Susan nor Mark was properly happy. They had no one to spend their money on, or share their time with at the end of a long working day, not that they had any time away from work. And then Susan and Mark met one another.

They were introduced on several occasions at works parties and although each found the other attractive neither made an effort to encourage any advance in the relationship.

Their introduction was rather unspectacular. Mark found Susan to be a little aloof and shallow, and she found him to be brash and cocky. It was above two years after their first introduction to one another that they were to work together on a substantial project.

Susan remembered the day vividly. It had been April the fifth; she still had the diary the meeting was marked in. The day had been a mix of weathers, rainy spells followed by sun and even a slight flurry of snow. Susan remembered the weather specifically, due to the fact she had been stood in it for above half an hour waiting for Mark to arrive.

They had only briefly spoken on the telephone to arrange a meeting place, outside Sheffield town hall at eleven o'clock. Mark had said that from there he would take Susan to a place that they could conduct their work.

She had been fuming when he had arrived, with his unkempt appearance and obvious lack of organisation, his papers spilled from his portfolio, she had been more than a little affronted by him.

He had made some brief apology for his lateness, but had made no specific excuses which had further annoyed Susan who prided herself on her timekeeping and efficiency.

If the job at hand had not been so important to her company she would have turned and left him, stood there by himself struggling with his overstuffed brief case, but she was far too professional for that.

"So," she had said through gritted teeth "where would you like to hold this meeting?"

Mark had simply winked, grabbed her hand and guided her gently through the town. Susan had been taken aback by his forwardness but somehow couldn't bring herself to let go of his warm hand, which softly enveloped her now cold one.

After a brief walk they arrived at a small café that Susan must have walked past a thousand times and never noticed. The windows she noted were a little greasy and though the chairs looked comfortable they were in need of reupholstering. A man was stood by the door taking deep pulls on a scented cigarette and the woman at the counter looked leathery and tired. Susan would have never stepped foot in this establishment normally, but she was being pulled forward by this odd man and had very little choice in the matter.

He sat and dropped his portfolio onto a round table, spilling papers and sketches all over it. Susan winced as she saw a rather beautiful sketch tumble onto a suspect sticky mark on the table top.

"Here we are then." Mark smiled widely and Susan felt her distaste for him tangibly begin to fade against her will.

The meeting went by in a flash. Susan very quickly warmed to Mark, because despite his brash approach he was amazing at his job and extremely determined and head strong. Mark warmed to her to when he realised that her abruptness and obsessive diligence was a cover for a million faults she saw in herself.

They worked incredibly well together, his spontaneity and her strict perfectionism pulled at the reigns of each other and after the meeting ended they both knew they couldn't quite give up this feeling they shared when together.

They set another date to meet for work and made sure that it would be a little more relaxed. As they waited for "drinks on Friday night" with each other they spent the week texting silly moments from their days and speaking on the telephone, under the guise of important work but secretly just wanted to know each other better.

Of course they met for drinks on the Saturday and spend near to no time talking about work. Susan told him of her fear that she would end up like her parents, which she had never spoken about before. Mark told her that he was afraid he would always be alone. They complimented each other as much socially as they did in work and they each had the night of their lives, a night which neither wanted to end.

Mark walked Susan home to her flat and found that it was only moments away from his, and it turned out Susan walked past him every day to work. He joked that it was fate, and she raised an eyebrow and said it was coincidence. He walked her to the door ad felt that awkward clichéd moment that happens at the end of a good night with someone of the opposite sex. He leaned in to kiss her and she leaned in to him to. The kiss began softly and almost polite, but neither pulled away, and before long they were locked in a passionate embrace.

Susan, who was never one to be swept away with fancy, would later swear that this early moment was when she fell in-love with him.

It didn't take long before they were practically inseparable and for the first time truly happy.

Now, over a decade on, life was very different for them both.

After only a year together they sold Mark's flat and they lived together at Susan's. Of course they had their ups and downs but quickly decided that they wanted to marry.

Even though they could have afforded something spectacular and Susan had always imagined a lavish day of glamour, they opted for a small ceremony with family and a few friends.

It was more important to simply be married than it was to have some frivolous day of expense and it was perfect.

Susan remembered seeing her fathers face as he walked her down the aisle to the altar. His eyes dewy and sparkling from the tears of pride he was holding back so well.

For the first time in her life Susan saw her father in a completely new light. All those years she had spent her life thinking that her father had wasted his time, finding a wife and raising a daughter, but she had been wrong. There had been nothing wrong with his choices. He had been happy; she could tell in his face that he was a man with no regrets. She felt a wave of embarrassment rush through her and it was hard to hold back the tears of shame that she had for judging her parents so wrongly.

Not long after the honeymoon they discovered they were to have their first child, something which initially terrified Susan, but with the help of Marks enthusiasm became a hugely exciting prospect.

After much debating The Johnson's decided that it was time to leave the hustle and bustle of Sheffield and begin a more simple life in the countryside. After months of looking for the perfect place, they decided to invest in a farmhouse that was located in a remote hamlet just outside of Chesterfield.

The outside of Pottery Cottage was stunning; a real chocolate box cottage. Wooden slanting gables, ivy covered walls and an English garden full of wild blossoms that smelt exquisite all year round.

They knew they were going to buy it before they even got inside, and so when they did they saw beyond the low roof, small misshapen rooms and cracking plaster. They would have bought it even if it had been condemned; because they knew it was simply their home.

Mark had never felt like that about property before, he had always been a bit of a nomad and home was where you hung your hat, but he knew instinctively that he would spend the rest of his life here and be happy until the day he died.

After buying Pottery Cottage, Mark and Susan had planned to renovate it themselves but didn't get the chance. The purchase took longer than expected and baby Claire Alice Johnson, six pounds and four ounces, was born before they got the chance. So for the sake of their sanity they hired contractors to do all the work, which ended up only taking a few months. With the renovations the old farmhouse was stunning. They didn't touch the structure so they wouldn't lose any character and they remained in keeping with the style, a dramatic change from their minimalist apartments in the city.

They even made an annex off the kitchen so that friends could visit for weekends and not feel pestered by the family.

No one had ever stayed though; their old friends still relics of their old lives with no free time, nor desire to relax in the countryside.

Once they were settled in Susan and Mark really adapted to the rural life.

Mark decided to start working from home so that he wouldn't miss out on the raising of his daughter and he helped out more that Susan had expected. He thrived in the role of a parent and this only fuelled Susan's deep love for him more. Susan became a full time Mother but helped out with Mark's work. This lifestyle had never been their dream or plan but it was working out wonderfully and she was happier than she had ever felt before.

The change showed even in Susan's appearance. Where she had worn her dark hair slicked back she now wore it long and free with its natural waves un-straightened. Her once heavily made up face rarely saw a makeup brush. She was proud of her natural rosy cheeks and soft brown eyes. She even held herself differently. Instead of an uptight brash stance she had become softer and more welcoming. She preferred herself this way. In general the simple life suited her well even though she had gained soft womanly curves and wore comfortable tee shirts and trainers instead of her old uniform of structured suits.

When Claire was two Susan and Mark decided to try for another baby and within a year Thomas Jack Johnson, seven pounds, was born.

Everything was as perfect as could be, until three years ago when Tom was three and Claire was six. Susan's mother fell suddenly ill. Susan moved back temporarily into her family home to help with caring for her mother who had contracted pneumonia. She still felt guilt for thinking of her parents badly in her younger years and hoped that her helping them in this awful time would serve as some penance.

Susan's parents had struggled to conceive a child and had been in their late thirties when they finally had their only child. Now they were in their seventies and her mother, Alice, was particularly frail. Despite the past, in recent years Susan had become increasingly close to her mother and father and was finding it difficult to cope with her mother's drastic decline in health.

Within a short month Alice passed away, leaving Susan inconsolable for many months to follow. Her father, Jack, began to act strangely and lose his short-term memory, which only added to Susan's anguish.

Jack and Alice Robinson had been married at the age of nineteen and had always been together. Alice's death was hard for her husband to deal with.

He refused to throw away any of Alice's belongings. He didn't even want to wash up the last cup Alice had drunk from. His house got into a terrible state, he barely had enough strength to get out of the bed, and on occasions didn't. Susan was at her wits end and full of inconsolable misery.

It was unbearable for the entire family, including Mark, Claire and Thomas. After much careful thought and deliberation with the children Mark suggested Jack came to live with them as they had more than enough room and he was fond of his father-in-law.

Susan was pleased with the idea, and although Jack put up some small resistance, at first, everyone decided that his moving in would be for the best. Even though he decided to keep his old house and leave it exactly as it had always been he finally started life in the annex at Pottery Cottage.

With the bustle of the move and the slow recovery of Jack's memory Susan began to get back to her old self and things began to become good again.

Three years on and life had never been better. Jack was back to his old cheerful state, reminding Mark of the grandfathers from Werther's Originals adverts.

Susan and Mark's business was thriving. They now had employees to do the grunt work leaving more time for them to spend with their kids but plenty of work to keep them from going insane with too much kid's television and finger painting.

It had even got to the point Susan didn't mind the constant stack of laundry and washing up, well almost.

Chapter Two

"Claire, come and pick up these dirty wellies and give them a good rinse! Tom, set the table!" She yelled, not even bothering to look up from the meal she was preparing.

After some cajoling the kids did as they were told while Mark went to find Jack in the garden. That was another good point in having her father living with them; the garden was always Chelsea Flower Show worthy, even in the middle of winter like now.

Jack was at the bottom of the frosty garden, pottering in the little shed. He loved that shed, said it was his haven.

"Alright Pop's?" He asked,

Jack looked up from painting an ornamental bird that he had bought cheap from a bring-and-buy fete at Claire's school.

"Ee, not to bad lad? You?"

Mark smiled "I've been sent to summon you for dinner"

Jack tutted and put down his delicate paintbrush. He looked at his watch.

"Crikey, I din't think it were that late. I better get me rear in gear!"

Mark left the old man packing his things away and went back into the house. Susan had almost finished preparing the food.

"Do you want a hand with anything, duck?"

Susan rolled her eyes, "What a good time ask, now that I have finished everything. You do have a knack!"

He pulled her towards him and kissed her on the forehead.

"We all have a talent my love! I'll round the kids up"

He headed into the dining room to find Claire on the floor being tickled into submission by her younger brother.

"Come on you pair; get sat down its going to be ready any second"

Tom stopped tickling Claire, and she took her opportunity to give him a swift but friendly punch in the ribs

"Daaaaaaad!" He yelled "Claire hit meeee!"

"Nobody likes a tattle tale Tom, and if you can't handle your sister, woe betides your future relationships!"

Claire and Tom came to the table, nudging and arguing under their breath the whole way.

"If you pair don't pack it in you can go to bed with no food!"

Back in the kitchen, Jack came rattling in leaving a trail of snowy wet boot prints behind him and hanging his dripping coat up over Claire's brand new school shoes.

"Dad!" Susan nagged as she carried their food through from the kitchen into the dining room. "Claire's only just tidied the kitchen floor".

"I'll sort it out in a bit" he said, looking at the prints. "It's easier to clean up when it's dry anyway, isn't it kids?"

Tom giggled. "You're in trouble, Granddad".

"Nowt new there then" Jack said winking at his grandson.

Susan put down a bowl of steaming mashed potato and looked sternly at her father before going to fetch the remaining serving dishes piled high with food.

"Wash your hands, green fingers; you're not setting a good example for the kids, eating with dirty mitts".

Jack stood up and began to slope off to the kitchen muttering loud enough for all to hear in his broad Yorkshire accent. "I don't eat wi me dutty mitts. I eat wi cutlery".

The children giggled as their mother rolled her eyes. She sat down at the head of the table and waited for her father to rejoin them.

After a few moments he did, still wiping his freshly washed hands on a tea towel he placed over his knee and they all tucked in to their food, hungrily, nobody saying a word as they chewed away contentedly. The only sound that could be heard over the mealtime symphony was the crackling of a dying log fire and the ticking of the grandmother clock that had belonged to Alice.

After about ten minutes of nothing but satisfied lip smacking, Mark finally spoke up.

"How's the weather Jack? I'm surprised you can do anything out there with the ground's not frozen over".

Jack finished chewing the mouth full he had and swallowed it before speaking.

"It will be soon. Snow's just started coming down thick and fast. It were still a bit damp from yesterday's rain but I wouldn't be surprised if we end up snowed in be mornin'"

Claire smiled widely, looking up from her food for the first time.

"Cool!" She looked to her mother; mouth still stuffed with semi-chewed food. "Can we build another igloo?"

Susan looked up to find everyone was now looking at her hopefully. She rolled her eyes again.

"Go on then, but you're not all sleeping in it this time! You had me worried sick all night. I didn't sleep a wink".

Mark smiled, remembering the last igloo adventure.

"We didn't sleep either; someone..." he gestured at Tom "... kept needing a wee every five minutes".

They all chuckled at Tom, who being the youngest was always a source of amusement. He just grinned cheerfully, the image of his father, and continued to munch away happily.

"And Granddad kept farting!" Claire chimed in.

"Claire!" Susan exclaimed at her daughters crude language, but her chides went unnoticed beneath everyone else's giggles, and Susan couldn't help herself but to chuckle along.

"Better out than in, eh lass"

Suddenly there was a loud, urgent knock at the door, which resounded throughout the house and made everyone jump and stop giggling. The adults all looked at each other wishing they didn't have to be the one to answer it. They didn't get many uninvited visitors being so isolated and begrudged anyone unexpected, especially during mealtimes.

Mark gave in first, "I suppose I'm closest", and went to the door, which was just in the hallway behind the door to Mark's right. Though the door was close no one could see the visitor so the rest of the family speculated as to who would be calling at such a late hour.

The door opening echoed in the hall and everyone heard a scuffling noise follow.

Susan began to feel a little uneasy as there were no voices, only a loud thud and a throaty sound, which seemed to issue from Mark, followed by the sound of something soft hitting something hard. Susan looked at her father with confusion and fear, but his eyes were positioned steadfastly on the open dining room door.

All of a sudden a man dishevelled looking and angry, burst through the dining room door causing every member of the family to jolt back with surprise.

Susan took the man in as he glared at them all for a moment. The features on his face were ferocious and tainted with evil. His body was tall and slender and he was obviously all muscle stretched over a wiry frame. He was six foot tall or more, yet he seemed smaller, crouched and irritating like an itch. However behind his shallow pale blue eyes there was a stillness that made him seem more violently menacing than his stature or demeanour could do alone. His dark hair was incredibly dishevelled and hung in short greasy curls. His whole facade made him appear uncared for and uncaring in return.

His sallow face was twitchy and angry, yet not unattractive. Susan's hindbrain noted she would have found him, if neatened up and calmed, very eye catching and handsome, not completely unlike Mark, but far more feral.

His clothes didn't quite fit him properly, they were baggy and worn, odd denim things that didn't match or suit him. Susan noted he wore no shoelaces in the heavy black boots that adorned his sockless feet.

He stared at everyone looking almost more surprised to find them staring back at him than they were to see him invading their family home.

Susan, feeling the need to say something, prepared herself to speak but before she had the chance the volatile intruder dashed forward and grabbed Claire around the throat ferociously yanking her out of her seat and flinging her in front of his body. He pulled a knife from his belt and held it to the small girl's terrified face.

Jack stood up quickly and with purpose causing his chair to fall backwards with the force of his movement.

"Hey, who do you think you are? Put down my granddaughter!"

The man's face twisted into a cacophony of pure rage, he flung Claire about like she was as light and limp as cloth as he approached the table.

"Shut the hell up, old man" he shouted through gritted teeth and tight lip. Barely audibly he added "or I'll shoot your fucking head off" as he grabbed a gun from the waistband of his trousers and pointed the barrel shakily between Jack's eyes.

He looked so terrorizing, with a knife in one hand, pressed painfully against Claire's increasingly tear soaked cheek, and in the other a gun unsteadily pointing at Jack's head.

Susan wondered if this man was scared for some reason, because he shook so violently, but it soon became apparent that it wasn't fear that was making him shake, but pure fury and possibly insanity.

She decided the best thing she could do was to try and cooperate with him, otherwise she was sure he was desperate enough to kill them all.

"What do you want from us?" she asked tentatively unsure if she was making a false move by trying to communicate with this beast.

The man looked at her shocked with wide eyes and a twitching expression, his mind visibly ticking. In a calm, crackly voice he began to speak again, slowly and with definite purpose.

"I need somewhere to hang out for a while. I didn't realise this place had been bought".

Jack suddenly yelled, making Susan jump. "Then why did you knock?" he demanded, frustrating Susan who felt sure the maniac would hurt her daughter if her father angered him further.

The man, still pointing the gun at Jack, twitched his eye.

"You" he yelled, flicking the gun sideways as he spoke "Go into the kitchen. You" he pointed at Susan "go into your bedroom and wait. Don't try anything or…" He dragged Claire towards her brother and eyed them eerily, "I'll make these suffer for it".

Susan petrified and almost in tears ran out of the dining room and into the hall that lead to the stairs. She paused for a moment stunned by the sight that lay before her. There sprawled across the floor, bleeding from his head, yet still taking shallow breaths lay Mark. A dark plume of glistening blood was gradually swelling from above his temple where a large gash was shockingly shimmering; Susan began to bend down to him, the urge to hold him untameable.

The intruder appeared around the door, "I said to your room, now!" He yelled so vehemently it made Susan's ears hurt "I'll take care of him! Do as I say!"

Fear coursing through every vein, Susan ran up the stairs and into her bedroom, her head swimming and unfocused. She walked to her bed, listening intently for any sound that would tell her how her family were, and waited shaking on her bed, the image of her husband blinding her to any other vision.

What had he done to Mark? What was he going to do to her? She didn't dare think on it too much, but her mind was running away. She could feel a pain in her chest and her thoughts seemed to scream at her. "You're going to die!" She could see it now, he was going to rape her and kill her and leave her bleeding and in pain on her own bed, the bed she had conceived her children in. She already felt violently sullied by the mere thought of her fate.

The dread for the end of her life gripped her body and she quivered uncontrollably, rocking back and forth in the vein attempt to calm herself and see some way out of this awful situation. She tried to shake the racing pictures from her mind but she could not! She tried to tell herself that this was all some bad dream, but she knew that it wasn't.

Unexpectedly the image of her little girl being dragged around like a ragdoll by that maniac flicked into her mind and brutally shocked her out of herself pity.

What was he going to do to her babies? She realised that she didn't care what he did to her, as long as he didn't hurt Claire and Tom. She would let him do anything if he left her family alone. He could gladly take every penny she had worked so hard to earn and every stick of furniture she had spent so long choosing with her husband. None of that mattered if the people she loved were Okay.

After what seemed several long minutes the man who was keeping her hostage arrived, a shadow looming in her bedroom doorway. She hadn't noticed before but he stank of pungent stale sweat. The smell preceded him as he entered the room and Susan could taste it right to the back of her throat. She wanted to gag at the tangy taste, but she did not dare. Her stomach turned and it took every fibre of her will to keep from retching.

All this proved to make this man; slowly entering her sanctuary, seem more real somehow. His odour seemed to grip her as he moved purposely around the room, eyes searching the walls and skirting boards, Susan assumed for a telephone socket.

She felt she should continue to cooperate. If she could keep him happy then perhaps he would be kind to her, as kind as a heartless brute could be at least.

"There isn't a phone up here; we only have one in the lounge." The man didn't acknowledge her but continued to stalk around the room like a heavy shadow. Susan couldn't help herself asking the question, she had to know. "Please," she began "Are my family alright?"

The man turned to her swiftly, anger etched in every line on his face.

"They're in their room downstairs. I won't touch them again as long as you behave".

He drew the curtains and turned on the light, swooping round the room like some rancid bat.

"How far away is the town?" he asked abruptly as he turned back to the window and looked cautiously through a corner of the curtain out onto the yard, which led to the street in front of the house.

Susan was confused but a jolt of excitement hit her in the throat, maybe he was planning to leave soon.

"A few miles, ten minutes by car" she babbled, desperate for him to go away and terrified for her own life. Ours is on the drive if you want to use it".

He turned back on her. "You talk too much." He twitched as he spoke. "Be quiet, I need to think." He perched on the end of the bed; as if not quite part of his own body "You've all landed me in shit." He blurted out "You weren't supposed to be here".

Susan wanted to ask him who he was and why he was there, but she didn't dare say another word. He was scaring her more and more by the second. The longer she sat silently on her bed, the worse the thoughts whizzing around her head became. She was sure she was going to be hurt, if not raped or murdered. She swallowed down a thick painful lump of fear in her throat and choked back prickly tears.

She began to shiver and, trying to distract her desperate mind, she watched the man. His movements were twitchy and mechanical. Every muscle under his thin dirty skin was tensed visibly, making his face strangely contorted.

His clothes were not tatty but they were worn in places and filthy. He looked as though he had been wearing them for days. For the first time Susan really noticed his clothes. Previously she had been concentrating more on the man's face and attitude.

He was wearing a light blue shirt with a patch sewn on the breast pocket. He wore jeans which had scuffs here and there, and his sturdy black shoes had no laces. Susan mused he looked like a convict, not quite daring to believe he could be. The man smelt as though he had been wearing these garbs whilst very active, as though he had worn them whilst running and sweating. Her whole bedroom had begun to smell bitter and tangy like rusting metal.

Susan continued to flick her eyes to her alarm clock. Time seemed to either leap forward in blinks, or slink slowly past as though unwilling to move on.

After almost two hours of anxious panic and fear, watching this man erratically jerk the curtains, he unexpectedly spoke, quick and harsh.

"Stay where you are. I'm going to the toilet." Barely moving he seemed to nonetheless impose down on her suddenly like a pressing thick shadow, his voice turning from angry and demanding to hushed and menacing. "If you even move at all I'll shoot every last one of them". He jolted his arm to the door indicating her family beyond and then lurched to the en-suite beside Susan and slammed the door behind him.

Deciding it would not be wise to disobey her captor Susan instead listened intently, not for him but for her family. She didn't hear a single sound beyond the man in her bathroom and the soft homely noises she was used to.

Realisation dawned that her family had probably been bound and gagged while she waited for him here. That would explain why the man had taken so long to follow her up to this bedroom. He must have decided to keep her to use for some reason, or perhaps her cooperation of earlier had earned his trust.

Susan on hearing the toilet flush snapped her out of her own thoughts. It was quite surreal. She and Mark had watched films with hostage situations before. Horror films, Zombie flicks. She had even enjoyed them before, though she knew she no longer would.

No one ever needed the toilet in these films. No one ever did anything so mundane, and therefore somehow it made everything so much scarier because this was real. This wasn't a film. The chances weren't for her just because she was the leading lady. Anything could happen.

She could feel her skin burning up. Her heart was pounding through her entire body, the back of her neck felt as though it was on fire and she could feel her cheeks flushing with heat. She felt as though bubbling cold water was welling up behind her breast. A burning sickness began to consume her entire body from head to toe and her eyes began to roll back into her head as everything started to fade away through grey into black.

Chapter Three

Susan began to reawaken. She rolled over between warm sheets, feeling sleepy awareness wash over her.

It was morning. She half opened her eyes to be greeted by the dawn sunlight that could only come from the bright reflection of rays on snow. Her bed felt cosy and warm. She didn't want to wake up she was so relaxed and enveloped in comfort. She embraced this calm like a big hug.

Then Susan remembered the man. For a second her heart leapt, it had all been some terrible nightmare. As she began to calm, taking in deep thankful breaths, her heart stopped again. She could still easily smell that cold harsh stench that had arrived with him and made it impossible to forget his invasive presence.

She woke up fully with a start but she could sense no one was in the room with her. She sat up, hoping he had gone while she had been unconscious, flinging her feet off of one side of the bed hopefully. As her eyes began to focus in the morning light she caught sight of him, crouching in the corner by the door. Despite half expecting to see him Susan jumped.

"In a hurry to leave?" he asked, with a sly lilt to his voice.

"What happened?" Susan asked, eyes prickling with tears again.

She realised she was in her nightdress and began to feel absolutely struck through with terror again. "What have you done to me?" she asked, a tingling shudder washing up her body.

The man smirked, or at least half his face broke into a sly grin.

"Don't flatter yourself love! I haven't done a thing to you. I got you ready for bed. You were too hot. I didn't want you being ill". Susan almost felt flattered until he added, "I don't know if I'll need you".

He flinched as though ashamed and looked down to his feet. Susan could sense that he hadn't wanted to say too much. He had told her he didn't want her ill so he obviously wasn't going to kill her. Relief swept over her as this thought consumed her. She could literally feel the fear slowly ebb out of her body.

The man seemed to be getting angry with his self though. Susan didn't want this. As long as he was calm she had a chance of surviving this awful situation intact.

"Thank you". She tried, praying he would take pity on her.

The man's features twisted as though a battle of emotions was ensuing behind his eyes. Gradually his lips curled into a smile, which made the man's face even grizzlier than ever.

"You're welcome," he added in a voice grizzlier than his face.

He abruptly propelled himself upwards and forwards toward her. At first Susan thought he was going to attack her but he breezed past the bed and towards the window. He pulled the curtains apart with one savage motion then suddenly stopped stock-still and peered out silently for some time. Susan felt incredibly uncomfortable. Conscious of her body and the fact that this terrifying stranger had seen her and touched her while she lay passed out and vulnerable only added to her fears. He may have done nothing beyond re dress her but even if he hadn't she felt violated, disgusted and impossibly scared.

Susan swallowed down a rising ball of panic in her throat and decided to try and gain the man's confidence. Not knowing where to begin she allowed her mouth to overtake her brain as she spoke

"My name's Susan. What's your name?"

The man muttered something under his breath that Susan didn't quite hear.

"I'm sorry I didn't hear".

"Jimmy" he repeated, irritation growing but still not turning away from the window.

Susan swallowed hard again, not knowing whether to continue with her line of questioning or give up. She sat for another long stretch of time before deciding to ask Jimmy why he was in her house. Unsure how to ask she opted for the old favourite of the movies.

"What do you want from us?"

"I've ... just got out of jail and I need some place to hi... stay for a while. I used to hang out here as a kid when it was derelict. I didn't know anyone had moved in".

Susan thought she sensed an opportunity to persuade Jimmy out of her house, but knowing her attempts were in vain she still tried.

"If you need somewhere to stay there is a Travel Inn in town. It's not very expensive. I can give you the money to stop there if you need it".

Jimmy turned from the window in a swift motion and Susan found his face mere inches from hers. He was leaning so far over her she had to lay back on the bed to prevent him from touching her.

Even without actual body contact Susan felt molested, and when Jimmy's knee brushed against her inner thigh she felt as though his greasy body was raping her. She cringed and tried to curl away from what she believed imminent, but instead Jimmy spoke in an oddly calm yet commanding voice.

"Nice try! As soon as I leave this place you'll call the pigs. And besides that..." Jimmy leered, the fingers of his fetid breath curling into Susan's lungs. She saw his eyes briefly flick over her body. "... We're snowed in. Look!"

He lifted his right arm and pointed his finger to the window but didn't move any of the rest of his body. Susan remained perfectly still.

"I trust you," she uttered, not daring to take her eyes from Jimmy's stubbly dark lips.

"Look!" he exclaimed so viciously Susan flinched, tensing the muscles in his thin arm to the point where this small movement made the mattress rock beneath her.

Because Jimmy remained unmoving Susan had to slide out from beneath him awkwardly to get to look out of the window. This caused the hem of her nightdress to ride up her legs and expose her thighs. She saw Jimmy's eyes rest on the inside of her left leg. His tongue slid over his bottom lip seedily, causing a prickly shiver to crawl up Susan's back.

She managed to pass him, pull down her nightdress and look out of the window. Despair filled her vision. The ground was deeply covered in snow. The flurry of pure white flakes had caused a sea of soft snow that consumed the landscape. It must have been at least two feet thick; it was halfway up the car so Susan couldn't see the wheels at all.

The beauty of the chocolate box scene was juxtaposed with the horrors inside her home. Susan ordinarily loved the snow. She, and her family, would wrap up warm before going outside and playing all day. She had planned to make a warming stew for lunch while the children continued to enjoy themselves outside.

She had looked forward to watching them out of the kitchen window as she prepared the vegetables.

Mark would have built a huge log fire in the fireplace they'd uncovered together and had restored when they first moved in. Jack and the kids would take off their cold, wet gloves and socks and hang them on the fireguard while they ate.

After this they would have gotten out the sledges from the shed. Jack had made them a few years before and they were fantastic and fast. Susan's fears dissipated, only to be replaced by a deep sad regret.

This awful man had taken that wonderful day away from her. He had robbed her of the memories her family could have made together. He had locked her up in her bedroom, a place that should have been a safe sanctuary, and kept her away from her children, husband and father. She felt a large, warm tear break from her lashes and roll down the side of her nose, hitting her quivering lip and leaving a warm, salty tang on her taste buds.

"My children" she said with no emotion.

"I told you last night" Jimmy grunted, "I won't touch them again as long as you do what you're told".

At that she felt her stomach lurch. She had never finished her dinner last night and she was famished. As she put her hand on her stomach it gave an audible rumble causing Jimmy to smile and Susan to be repulsed at the sight of his filthy leer.

"Hungry?" he asked inanely.

Any other situation and Susan would have rolled her eyes and had no time for this stupid man's impertinence, but she didn't put him down for fear she would set him off and cause him to do harm to her, or worse, her family.

"I'll make you some breakfast" he said to Susan's great surprise.

Prior to this he remained on the bed. Now he suddenly stood upright and tall before he swiftly left the room and headed down the stairs. Unsure if he was really going to make food and desperate Susan dropped to the floor, squashing her ear deep into the carpet and listened intently to hear some sign that her family was still safe. She could hear things bashing about in the kitchen and ... voices. "Thank God" she thought as her heart jumped with joy and relief. They were alive. She strained her hearing even further but still she could only make out monotone indistinguishable mutterings. At least it was something. She could hear the clattering of the pots and pans then heavy footsteps. Jimmy must have been going into the living room, perhaps her father or Mark was there. The steps turned back and became louder. He was back in the kitchen.

Susan heard Jimmy bash down what she imagined to be four plates and thought of Mark. If he was eating breakfast he must have not been too injured from the scuffle last night. Again some indistinguishable mutterings issued from the kitchen before Jimmy's thudding steps thumped into the annex. He must have been taking someone their breakfast. After a brief silence the mutterings and clattering returned.

Eventually Jimmy's heavy boot clad footsteps ascended the stairs giving Susan just enough warning to jump back on the bed and act as though she hadn't moved a muscle. Jimmy barely looked at her as he passed her a bowl of cereal and went back to his vigilant gaze out of the window in deep thought.

Susan consumed her cereal in silence. It was hard to swallow as she ate and every spoonful of the cornflakes hurt as it passed down her throat. She could feel the prickly sensation of tears forming in her eyes again, though she tried, with no avail, to hold them back.

As if sensing her weakness, Jimmy turned to her and gave her a cruel grin.

"Something wrong with your breakfast?"

The sound of his now slick and oily voice caused Susan to wince and the spoonful of cereal she was about to swallow stuck painfully in her throat. She had no chance of holding the flood of tears back now as they washed down her face in sporadic torrents of salty heat.

"Please" she begged shamelessly, food debris spilling from her mouth "Please, please let me see my babies. Please, please, they'll be so frightened".

She wiped her milky chin and swallowed hard.

Jimmy looked back out of the window with strangely glazed eyes. For a moment Susan thought he may begin to cry too, but if he had been about to he was holding it back well, his eyes hardened before he turned and looked at her again.

"They're tied up right now," he said with a throaty, snorting laugh, proud of his little joke.

Susan gave in to her emotions and slumped down, hiding her sobbing face behind her quaking hands. She couldn't bring herself to look up but she could hear the soft padding of Jimmy's footsteps over the carpet as he approached her bed. The mattress dipped slowly to Susan's left as Jimmy lowered his body onto the bed, which creaked under his weight though he was very slim. He put his cold hand tenderly onto her shoulder making her jump and look up.

Susan was so instantly shocked by this moment of unexpected tenderness. Jimmy's touch was warm, and his rough worn skin complemented his gentle caress. Though feeling indecent a strange urge to embrace him swept over Susan as she sat beside this terrible stranger in her nightdress. She felt drawn to him, as though an unspoken, inexplicable bond fixed her to him. Though the thought of him made her skin crawl, she needed this fragile contact. Susan closed her eyes as the need to be held began to consume her very bones.

Then Jimmy spoke, and Susan felt the powerful grip of human contact wash rapidly from her.

"Perhaps..." he said slowly, "When the weather clears we'll need some things from town. You can fetch them. If you do as you're told and don't tell a soul I'm here", he removed his hand and Susan noticed his torn, pensive expression, "you can see them. But if you're as much as a minute longer than I say, or you don't have everything I tell you to get, I'll kill them, all of them! Do you understand?"

Susan nodded painfully, yet with a shallow sense of relief and hope.

Slow hours passed but the snow remained. As time passed Jimmy became gradually calmer and more eager to talk although he still continued to silently stare out of the bedroom for ages, only moving to escort Susan to the en suite or to go downstairs to check on things.

He had gained no real trust for her and watched her eagerly. Even when he left the room she had no opportunity to escape. She cursed herself for her lack of bravery, but dared not do a thing to risk the lives of her family.

Every time he left her Susan felt far more terrified than when he was in the room with her because whenever she couldn't see him terrifying images of what he could be doing to her family flashed before her eyes.

Every few hours Jimmy would bring her some food, biscuits, cereal or sandwiches. He obviously wasn't domesticated.

Susan would watch him for great expanses of time, trying to work out his moods, thoughts and even his past. He was a complete mystery and his thoughtful silences made him not only frightening but also almost romantic. He could have been any of a thousand exciting things in a million exotic places. The longer Susan spent in his presence the more she became convinced that he wasn't really bad, perhaps misunderstood.

Deep down she knew he was unstable, but by keeping them alive he was showing that he had some moral compass, even if it was slightly out of tune.

"So!" He exclaimed, "Tell me about yourself".

By his tone Susan knew she had to obey.

The bedroom window looked out onto the side of the house and gave a good view right along the lane that lead into the town. Jimmy must be monitoring the roads. Susan didn't, for a second, believe Jimmy's story about being released from jail. He was on the run. Innocent people didn't hold a young family hostage, and as far as she knew ex offenders were returned their civilian clothes, rather than remain in the hardwearing denim prison fatigues. This obvious fact made Jimmy's brooding silences even tenser.

After hours of awkward silence the light outside had begun to fade. Susan forced herself to glance at her watch. It was almost six o'clock. The light must have remained so late due to the reflection of a full moon on the thick white snow. Once sun began to give way to night darkness descended quickly throughout the house and made Susan to fall into an increasingly deeper depression.

Hours passed, and though she felt immense exhaustion, Susan couldn't sleep. Her body ached. She had not left the bed for any longer than it took to use the bathroom and because of this she felt stiff and uncomfortable. The darkness had well and truly taken hold and still the hours passed in awkward, terrifying silence.

Susan kept trying to snatch moments of stolen sleep but every time she managed to begin to relax and close her eyes, some innocent tiny noise dragged her back and reality smacked her hard in the face. Seconds slipped past lazily, slowly seeping into minutes and congealing into hours.

Eventually grey light began to fill the room and Susan knew it was dawn. She looked at her watch, it was almost seven a.m. It had been above twelve hours in total silence.

Jimmy continued to pace relentlessly before the window. Susan's depression slowly began to be replaced by strengthening waves of frustration.

Why had this man chosen them?

Who was he?

Where was he from?

And what the *hell* was he glaring out of that *bloody* window for?

The questions echoed through her mind in an increasingly spinning angry spiral. She had to clench her teeth to stop herself from screaming out the questions she longed to have answered. This awful man had been an invader into her life for above a full day and she was beginning to feel infuriated by him.

"What are you staring at?" she yelled before thinking. Then as if the words had suddenly released all her frustration she lost her anger infused bravado and was awash with terror again.

Jimmy had spun round to look at her, eyes wide with shock. A tiny thin smile began to slither across his leathery face.

"There hasn't been a single car drive down this road since I arrived". His smile widened, he was toying with her, stringing her along. He wanted her to keep questioning him so that he could spoon-feed her like a child.

Susan's frustration returned, and this time it stayed, yet even so she couldn't keep herself from asking "So?"

Jimmy's smile remained, but his cheek twitched.

"So..." he began slowly, "... they can't be chasing me can they?"

"Who?"

Susan was totally consumed with rage. Her chest and throat burned with the pain of trying not to erupt from her emotions.

"The police". His smile began to fade, yet the twitch in his cheek continued to tick sporadically. "Who do you think?"

"I thought you'd been released" she spat with venom.

Jimmy turned back to the window as a slow insane laugh began to bubble up out of him. The anger in Susan ebbed a little, to be replaced by a tickling fear in her chest, but only for a second before fury returned with a new lustre.

"Of course no-one's come. The road'll be blocked with snow!"

Although Jimmy didn't move, he seemed to physically stiffen.

"So?" he said without looking at her.

"So no-one'll be able to get through. You couldn't even get up the drive. Mark usually clears the snow. The whole lane will be impossible to drive down until the snow clears".

Jimmy abruptly turned to her, a look of intense fear flashed across his face. Susan was confused.

"Surely you should be happy? The police can't get here until the snow clears".

Suddenly Susan felt a rise of hope and inspiration grip her. A thought formed behind her lips, before uncontrollably pushing its way out of her mouth in the form of a question.

"Why don't you run?"

Once the question escaped more words tumbled out after them, like an avalanche.

"If you leave now, by the time the snow clears you could be miles away".

The sickening smile swept across Jimmy's face again, causing the skin around his frosty green eyes to wrinkle.

"Nice try! If the roads are blocked I'm not going anywhere. They'll never look for me here. Looks like I landed myself in just the right place at the right time".

Susan's heart sank, but she couldn't give up. Her desperation took over her head and her voice bypassed her brain as she spoke, shocking herself.

"People will notice something wrong. People will miss us!"

This seemed to have an effect on Jimmy who moved away from the window.

"Who? Who will notice?"

He sounded unsure and frightened. Clutching at any hope she could find, Susan racked her brains.

"The neighbours", she spat out with a sudden new hope.

"They'll notice that Mark hasn't cleared the paths. They'll notice we haven't left the house".

Jimmy's eyes drifted about the room erratically and unfocused. For a moment he seemed disoriented and dazed by this new revelation. Then, with sharp abruptness, he snapped back

"Well then..." he seemed to regain control over his mind, "... you'd better show your face".

He moved sweepingly to the wardrobe and flung open the double doors to reveal all of Mark and Susan's clothes, which swayed on their hangers from the force of the opening door. Jimmy grabbed a sparkly top Susan had bought to wear at her cousin's wedding reception last year, and a pair of Mark's jeans. He threw them onto the bed beside Susan before turning to her underwear drawer and rummaging in her knickers.

She felt a wave of violation sweep through her. This man had been here for so long now she had forgotten how she felt scared for her own body. The thought of her babies had over powered her senses, but now as his filthy fingers passed over her delicate lingerie a feeling in the pit of her stomach overwhelmed her. He could overpower her and rape her and there was nothing she could do.

He added a pair of pants and socks to the pile of clothes on the bed.

"Get dressed," he grunted.

Susan looked at the mismatch of clothes.

"Those jeans aren't mine", she ventured.

Jimmy looked at her with an almost sarcastic expression on his face.

"I don't care," he said, so calmly it was chilling.

Susan picked up the sparkly top and looked at it for a moment but decided against changing into this first. She picked up her underwear and stood up out of the bed; aware that Jimmy's eyes followed her unashamedly. Holding her underwear in her hand and already feeling naked she looked up at Jimmy hoping he would spare her the indignity but knowing he was not that kind.

She could feel her cheeks redden and prickle with heat. Her eyeballs felt as though they were literally filling with warm tears. Her chest tensed as though a hand was gripping her heart and trying to hold her back.

Though she glared at her captor imploringly he showed no sign of empathy, if anything he was getting a kick out of her shame. With nothing left to do she pulled her nightdress down to cover the tops of her thighs as best she could. Painfully remembering that he must have already seen all the parts of her body he desired when he changed her into her nightdress but she couldn't bear those lust filled eyes on her body.

As she slipped her underpants down her legs she ventured another quick look up at Jimmy, who hadn't taken his eyes from her. His serpentine tongue slithered over his bottom lip disgustingly. Susan felt dirty. As quickly as she could she pulled on the clean pants, followed by Mark's jeans. Feeling momentarily better, the worst was over and she was nearly changed. If he hadn't done anything beyond watch her up to this point he wouldn't do anything now. She just had to get past this humiliation.

She picked up the sparkly shirt, there was nothing she could do but remove her nightdress, and thanked God he hadn't taken of her bra. She took off the nightdress and tried to replace it as quickly as she could. It wasn't easy, she was becoming clammy and flustered and entangles in the top's straps. The room was fairly cold, and the fresh crisp air was caressing her skin and emphasising her nakidity. Goose pimples rose all over her so aggressively it stung. It felt as though millions of hands were invading her skin and pulling her apart. Jimmy suddenly seemed closer, even though he hadn't moved. It felt as though even his shadow was leaning in and groping her.

After some awkward fumbling with her clothes she was finally she was dressed. She knew she looked ridiculous with her fancy top and her husband's over sized jeans, but she felt more comfortable than she had all day.

She looked back to Jimmy who looked away from her chest and to her face.

"You'll need a coat". His expression never changing.

"It's downstairs" she replied, her heart beginning to race. She may get a chance to see her family. She may even get a chance to make a run for it.

"Come on then". He began to walk out of the room and down the stairs. Susan followed, filled with the excitement of leaving her room and possible seeing Claire, Thomas, Mark and her father.

Chapter Four

They reached the bottom of the stairs, which opened up into the living room. The plates and food from the night Jimmy burst in were still on the table, now cold and stale. There was a milky layer of film over the tea that she and her father had been drinking that night.

"Where is everybody?" Susan asked imploringly.

"They're comfortable," he said without acknowledging her physically.

"Please, can I see them?" she begged.

Jimmy looked at her.

"They're in their rooms".

Susan reprimanded and felt incredibly frustrated. How did he expect her to do his bidding when she didn't even know if they were alive?

"So!" she said stubbornly. "I want to see my children. Now!"

Jimmy turned on her. His eyes filled with fury and his nostrils flared, but Susan wasn't backing down. Without them her life was meaningless. It wasn't courage pushing her to stand up to Jimmy, because she felt nothing, nothing at all beyond her desperate longing to see her little innocent children.

Jimmy looked strange; his face suddenly flushed and pink in the cheeks. His sage coloured eyes glazed over, as though he was near to tears. His eyes widened as he moved his face close to hers, his foul breath uncoiling up her nostrils.

"Fine".

The single syllable hit Susan like a train and she felt her entire body lose tension. She almost collapsed but knew she had to stay strong and keep going. Jimmy kept his entire body close to hers unflinching and menacing. His eyes flickered across Susan's face as though he was searching for something there. After a moment he spoke again, making her go weak kneed once more.

"But ... "he continued to glare at her "if you want to see them, you leave off asking about them until I'm gone. You do every damn thing I tell you, without fail, and without question from now on".

Susan didn't even have to think about the answer, she nodded in agreement immediately. Jimmy led her through the kitchen into the annex that had been converted for Jack to help him keep his independence. The children didn't usually sleep here, but they had a little playroom with a day bed. Jimmy must have mistaken this for their bedroom. Susan wasn't about to correct him.

They rounded the corner into the playroom. The floor was littered with the debris that comes with children. The toy box lids were up and they were almost devoid of toys.

Susan looked up at Jimmy, suddenly seeing a new side to him. He must have allowed Claire and Thomas to play. She was holding back happy tears as she looked to the day bed.

She could see Thomas' fluffy brown hair peeking out over the Noddy duvet. Claire was lying behind him, her arm over his chest protectively, her hair covering her face. They looked so peaceful. She longed to hold them. Unable to keep the tears from flooding down her face, she went to the bed, but felt Jimmy grab her arm. It was the first time she had felt him touch her and it took Susan by surprise.

His skin felt rough and oddly warm against her arm. He was strong, she could tell, yet he gripped her somehow gently. His eyes were watery again as he spoke in a whisper.

"Don't ... you'll disturb them" he said in a caring manner Susan could have never imagined him having.

Susan felt suddenly light and elated. Her children were here, inches away from her and comfortable. The man that had terrorised her was protecting them, keeping them comfortable and happy. The threat of him lost in an instant. The steely cold stare converted somehow into a sad, lonely veil. Susan needed desperately some human contact. The brief touch of his hand enforced this deep longing.

She threw herself in to embrace Jimmy, a strange compulsion beyond her control. She allowed her weakened body to fall vaguely limp against his strong, sturdy frame, as he held her tightly without hesitation. His warm hard body felt like an oasis of comfort against the bleakness of the few days that had proceeded.

He was taller than she and wider than his slender looking frame suggested. With his arms around her she was completely enveloped and it felt amazing.

She kept her eyes closed as tightly as their embrace and lost all track of reality, joyously lost in a world of warmth and comfort that she never wanted to leave again. After several minutes she felt Jimmy pull away and the spell was broken. As he gently released her, the warm contact his body had made to hers felt colder than ever before and she was alone again in a harsh situation she couldn't control.

She looked to the day bed and wiped her sodden face before looking at Jimmy. His cheeks were a warm pink, and his eyes, although free from tears, were full of a kind of bright emotion Susan would never have imagined finding there. Unexpectedly her heart skipped a little and she felt a warm tingling in her chest.

With this she felt more disturbed than ever before. Her husband was potentially wounded. She had not seen him in days and she was grotesquely attracted to this monster that was the cause of all her current woes. How could she feel such vile betrayal? She was repulsed by herself, yet she could no sooner prevent her feelings than she could have stopped herself from holding Jimmy as she had moments ago.

Silently Jimmy ushered Susan out of the playroom and back in to the kitchen. It was beginning to smell awful from the rotten, decaying food that had not been consumed.

Susan followed Jimmy outside and the cold hit her as if tiny shards of ice actually punctured the flesh on her bare arms. With a fierce shudder she spoke.

"I forgot my coat, I'll just get it. It's only in the pantry". She turned to fetch it but was harshly stopped in her tracks.

"No!"

Jimmy lunged towards her and pulled her back so sharply she fell back in to the prickly cold snow. She was taken aback by his sudden outburst and, although bitterly cold, was unable to move.

She remained lying shocked in the snow, while Jimmy with an uneasy sense of haste turned and walked away.

With the dampness of the melting snow beneath her warm body seeping through her jeans Susan was too scared to move. Within moments Jimmy returned carrying Susan's coat. Now looking a little sheepish, he held the coat for her to put on, just as you would a young child. Under his breath he mumbled what Susan took to be "Sorry". She stole a brief smile. Thomas behaved this way. He would have a tantrum before realising how silly he was and then he would be too ashamed to apologise. Susan found it inexplicably endearing. She couldn't help contemplating how this gentle man had come to be such a venomous brute when angered. Like some defenceless creature clawing out when trapped and scared. His hard abrupt attitude juxtaposed with the warm and caring temperament he hid beneath it.

As she worked away, clearing the flurried snow, she thought of him and what had made him this way. It repulsed her to feel it, but her heart fluttered at the thought of him. She tried to stop herself, but the memory of his strong body against hers made her feel excited, and yet her skin still crawled.

She was barely concentrating on the job of clearing snow from the path as her mind was consumed by the conflicting thoughts and feelings she was enduring. All she knew was the snow was heavy on the shovel and she was feeling hot and sweaty beneath her clothes. With her consuming thoughts and hard work she didn't notice Mrs Byron walking up from her farmhouse a little way down the lane.

"Hello love".

The little old ladies husky smoke gruffed voice made Susan jump so much she dropped the shovel on her foot, causing an explosion of hot pain.

"Hiya Dora" Susan replied through gritted teeth.

"Doesn't Mark usually do that dear?" Mrs Byron asked innocently.

Susan loved Mrs Byron. She had been as much an appeal to buying the house as anything else. She wasn't your usual little old lady. She hobbled about every day, rain or shine, doing little jobs on the farm. She smoked vanilla scented thin cigars and swilled Guinness from a can as she chatted over the gate.

When they had first moved in she brought them a basket full of homemade scones and a jar of homemade blackcurrant jam. It had all tasted terrible and the scones were rock hard but even Mrs Byron laughed about it.

Susan thought before answering her question. If she let Mrs Byron somehow know about Jimmy she could call the police. As this small plan began to formulate in her mind Susan saw a flash of silver in the corner of her eye, at the side of the house.

Her eyes flicked to the right and she saw Jimmy with a knife blade in his hand. He gave Susan a harsh stare as he twisted the knife threateningly so that it glinted in the dull light.

Would he kill poor Mrs Byron?

She had never done anything to him, but then neither had Susan and her family.

"He's sick, Dora." thinking fast, "a cold. Probably because of all this damn snow. The kids and Dad are moaning too. They've prescribed themselves bed rest and plenty of hot chocolate so muggins here gets to do all the running about". She forced a little laugh.

Mrs Byron rolled her eyes knowingly.

"Man flu. Yes, my Roy gets that when work's to be done. Do you need anything?"

Susan quickly looked back to the house although she could no longer see Jimmy she could sense his eyes on her.

"No thank you, you've got enough on with your Roy".

Mrs Byron smiled and gave a little wave as she toddled off back towards her own farmhouse saying as she went "too true dear, too true".

Susan looked back to the house, but saw no sign of Jimmy. She prayed he didn't think she had told Mrs Byron anything; else he may be hurting someone in the house, yet she didn't dare go back and check. If she suddenly abandoned her work to go inside it would look incredibly suspicious to her neighbours. Also she had promised Jimmy she would trust him from now on. She continued with her chore.

When she had finished she put away the shovel and headed back to the kitchen door, but before she could open it, Jimmy did. He looked sweaty and harassed. Susan went in to the kitchen expecting to see something changed, but it was all as it had been before she went out, only this time she could smell something unpleasant beyond Jimmy's musk.

"What's that smell?"

Jimmy looked suspicious.

"What smell?"

"I don't know" she replied before it dawned on her. "I think it must be the food. It's turned".

Without thinking she went to the sink to fill it with soapy water and wash the dishes.

"What are you doing?" Jimmy asked, somehow affronted.

"The pots" Susan informed him with some confusion.

Jimmy turned off the tap.

"Leave them" his tone harsh, "I'll sort it when I make tea" he added, trying to bustle Susan out of the kitchen.

"Why don't I make it?" She asked in the hope she could stay out of the bedroom a little longer and also hoping she might see her family. "I enjoy cooking," she added, hoping he wasn't going to turn again.

Jimmy's eyes shifted awkwardly as he thought for a moment, obviously tempted by her offer but in some inner turmoil.

"Alright" he looked at her, "but I'll help".

This odd, childlike comment touched Susan, until he added:

"Don't want you doing anything stupid".

Pots were bubbling on the stove, pleasant cooking smells were filling the kitchen and if Susan closed her eyes it felt almost normal again. Except, of course, for the grubby man who insisted on fetching her anything she needed from the pantry. It was sweet of him but simultaneously very irritating. When the food was cooked she began dishing up and made to take it in to the dining room.

"Where are you going with that?" asked Jimmy.

"I thought we could all eat at the table".

Jimmy took the plate from her hand, causing some of the stray peas to roll off it and onto the floor.

"Not likely. Get you all together and I stand no chance do I?"

He began heading to the annex with two plates.

"Don't even think about following me!"

And with that he was gone from view. Susan dished out Claire and Tom's food on plastic plates with Rupert bear on. The kids were getting too old for these now but Susan couldn't bear the thought that they would soon be growing out of these things and becoming young adults.

She looked with sadness at the small steaming plates. Her plan to get everyone together had backfired, but it didn't seem terribly maddening. At least she knew they would be getting a decent meal, and the fact Jimmy had taken a plate for Mark meant he couldn't be too ill to eat and that was a relief.

Jimmy returned and took away the plates for Claire and Tom without saying a word. With nothing to do until Jimmy came back Susan picked at the food on her plate as she waited for him to come back.

"Can we eat down here?" she asked, trying to avoid going back to her room. She felt safer downstairs. It was somehow less imposing.

"Alright" he said, carrying his plate into the dining room and sitting at the table. Susan followed him feeling like a child in a stranger's house. It was an odd feeling, and made her stomach churn, to the point where the food on her plate seemed like a challenge to eat. Nevertheless they both began to eat silently. Jimmy carelessly flicked on the television that was on the welsh dresser. Susan had always hated having a television in the dining room but her father had insisted on it. He always liked to watch countdown while he ate a sandwich in the evening. It was a simple thing that had always irritated her, but she would never let such a silly thing bother her now. She loved those silly little things her father did that silently niggled away at her. She missed his silly sense of humour and his daft little sayings. She wanted him to hold her and call her Princess and tell her that everything was okay. There was nothing she wouldn't give to have just five minutes with him now, a few moments to hold all of them.

Her father's dining room television was an old thing. He had owned it all of her life, if not longer. It took a long time to warm up, the sound starting almost a full half minute before the picture appeared, Susan would have bought something much nicer if she hadn't been so annoyed by its presence. If it had been up to her there would only be one television in the house.

"...aped convicted murderer James Bailey is still at large. Police are warning residents in Derbyshire to be vigilant and very wary..."

Susan's heart leapt into her throat and pumped harder than she had ever felt it in her life. Jimmy began trying to flick off the TV to no avail. Another of its quirks was that it wouldn't shut off until after the picture appeared. He was getting very frustrated punching his thumb on the remote, but Susan was enthralled by the information emitting from the television.

"... police warn Bailey is may be armed and is considered extremely dangerous. If spotted do not approach under any circumstances. Officers have commenced door-to-door enquiries in the hope of finding leads as to his whereabouts but are being hampered by the appalling weather conditions. In the mean time officers are asking residents to keep to a 7pm curfew for their own safety, and to, under no circumstances, allow their children to venture out alone.

"Bailey, who has served four years of a life sentence for murdering a young pregnant woman in a botched robbery at a Sheffield bank, was being transferred to a court hearing in Chesterfield for trial after causing a riot in which a fellow inmate, Michael Walters, was near fatally wounded when Bailey stabbed him in the neck with a home-made knife.

"On the journey from Her Majesties Prison Wakefield to North East Derbyshire & Dales Magistrates Court, Chesterfield, police lost control of the prisoner who managed to break free of his handcuffs and knock out two police officers. A third officer, Brian Elway was stabbed in the scuffle by the makeshift knife Bailey had managed to conceal about his person before the transfer operation began. Officer Elway was admitted into the Intensive Care Unit at the local hospital where his condition, believed to be critical, has not been released to the pre..."

Momentarily a picture of a man Susan had never seen before flicked up on the screen before it promptly flicked off completely. Susan had been so engrossed in the newscaster's words she had not noticed Jimmy stand up, go over to the television and pulled the plug out of the wall socket.

Susan was shaking as she looked up at Jimmy's reddened enraged face. Her question about whether he would kill Mrs Byron was washed away. He had viciously murdered a young mother to be, and near fatally wounded two other people, one of whom could be dying at this very moment. The original fears she felt for him returned in hot terrifying waves, pulsing from her head down to her feet. She tingled horribly all over.

The muscles in Jimmy's face tautened until his fury could not be doubted. It was blatant that he was so fumingly mad he could barely breathe, let alone speak.

Susan didn't dare move. She too could barely breathe, but due to her utter fear for her life. She now knew too much. It seemed Jimmy had wanted to maintain some form of mystery. The less Susan knew of him the more fearful she could be, but the truth she had just heard was far more frightening than she could ever have imagined.

Before the televisions revelations she had been hopeful that he didn't really have it in him to kill, and that his threats were idle bravado, but they weren't.

Why had he kept them alive? He could have killed them as soon as look at them. He had the weapons and he had the ability. Did he enjoy toying with her? Did he want something from them?

Why?

Susan burst into tears. She couldn't take it any longer. She couldn't bear feeling afraid, or missing her family. She couldn't bear the constant rise and fall of so many emotions, or the pain she was feeling physically and emotionally. She was exhausted, frustrated and in complete agony. As the flood of tears cascaded down her cheeks and rolled over her lips, Susan suddenly lost all care for herself. She knew she smelt from days of not washing, her nose was running and her face grimaced as she sobbed but she simply didn't give a damn.

"Just fucking kill me," she screamed desperately, deflating with a sigh that punctuated her words.

She looked up into Jimmy's face, which had altered almost out of recognition from before. It had slackened and become softer; Susan could see his kind side flooding out of his eyes. He seemed almost concerned as he stared at her unblinking.

"What?" His voice was soft, unlike Susan had ever heard it before. The tears, which had abated from Susan's eyes, redoubled.

"I said just kill me Jimmy. Please. I can't keep going any more". She spoke through wet sobs

Jimmy, in a smooth motion, moved across the room and sat down beside Susan, placing his hand on her shoulder. Susan half expected him to say "All in good time" but he didn't say a word. He just looked at her, directly in the eye, his mouth open, his bottom lip moving as though he wanted to say something but couldn't bring himself to form the words. He stayed this way for some time before abruptly standing up and going in to the kitchen leaving Susan completely alone. Susan broke into another flood of tears and sat silently sobbing for a while, her mind whirling with an array of desperate thoughts. She genuinely wished she was dead, It was simply too hard and she felt like she couldn't keep it together for another moment.

Tears washed in thick warm torrents down her face. She tried to pull herself together but the more she tried to focus the harder she cried. Susan tried to open her eyes briefly, and as she did they rested on a photograph of her family. It was a lovely photograph from their last holiday. It had been taken by a photographer that had been in the hotel and it carried wonderful memories.

She had to pull herself together. She took a deep sobering breath, and swallowed hard and began to wipe her sodden face with her sleeves. As she did so her eyes, again, fell on something that made her mind snap into focus. The telephone.

Jimmy had let down his guard and left her alone with the phone. She stood up and went over to it. She had expected to feel elated at the opportunity to begin an escape, but she didn't. She still felt completely numb. The only thing driving her forward was a morbid curiosity.

She picked up the handset and held it to her ear, but before the cold receiver had even touched the side of her face she could tell the familiar dialling tone was not there. She pushed a finger onto the number nine, but as she expected there was no bleep from the phone. The lines were down. She only felt the minimal amount of disappointment. She had wanted to call the police, but the need to know the reason for all this was so much more important. After all, she had seen the children and they weren't in any pain. Everyone was being given food and he obviously wasn't going to kill her. He'd had ample opportunity already and hadn't even tried.

Susan let the phone limply fall back onto the receiver, defeated. Jimmy returned from the kitchen and lazily slumped into his seat before rocking forward, leaning on the table with his head in his hands, his greasy brown hair curled through his fingers. He didn't look up as she approached and Susan wondered if he was crying. She watched him for a moment before saying one simple word.

"Why?"

Jimmy looked up. He wasn't crying as Susan had expected. Did he even have the ability?

He looked into Susan's face for a long time, showing no emotion beyond an inquisitive look about his eyes that scanned her questioningly. A small frown curled between his eyebrows.

"Why what?" His voice was crackly as though he was exhausted by his emotions too.

"Why everything? Why rob a bank? Why kill people?" She began to get hysterical. "Why stab a prisoner? Why escape? Why here? Why us? Why me? "Why?" she finished with yell and without reason or control she grabbed a plate of manky food from the table and flung it at the wall, where it shattered sending splinters of porcelain and putrid food flirting back at her. One of the small bits of shrapnel hit Susan in the neck causing a flash of stinging pain, which had the odd effect of calming her. She closed her eyes to shut out the pain as she raised her hand to the cut, which was already seeping warm, sticky blood between her fingers.

Susan felt a warm sensation on her back; it was Jimmy's hand. She flinched away from it instinctively, but he grabbed her by the shoulders and held her firmly.

"Listen to me!" he said, spinning her to face him so that his mouth was close to her ear and their bodies touched.

"Don't think that you can go round throwing plates in a temper..." His teeth were clenched as his jaw tensed again. "... While I pander to your every whim! Who do you think you are, demanding things from me?"

He shook her and his arms tensing as his temper rose.

"You might come out of this alive if you shut the hell up and do as you're told. Mess with me, bitch, and I won't think twice about slitting that pretty lilywhite neck of yours".

He moved his strong hand weaving his fingers into Susan's increasingly greasy locks. He tugged at her hair, pulling her head to the side as to take a closer look at the cut she had made on her neck. She felt scared for a moment, he was very strong and even though she resisted him she was malleable in his hands. He pressed his face into the nape of her neck and licked the droplet of blood that had formed in the fresh cut. Although she couldn't help thinking that the warmth and tenderness of his skin on hers was pleasant, she was still violently repulsed by his wet tongue slithering over her goose pimpled flesh. Her flesh tingled and tightened.

Filled with a new emotion she had never felt before, she flung him off of her with all the strength she could muster.

"Get your hands off me you filthy bastard!"

With her unexpected reaction Jimmy was so taken aback he momentarily lost his footing and backed into the table with a bump. He looked at her, surprised, but she continued:

"I don't care about me anymore! I can't keep doing this. I can't keep feeling this sickness in the pit of my stomach. It would be better if you just killed me now".

She looked at him, genuinely desperate to end everything and just be gone far away from this hellish prison he had created around her.

"So I'll damn well do as I please" she said reaching past him for a second filthy plate, "because dying doesn't scare me anymore!" and she meant it! She meant it as she pulled her arm back. She meant it as she took aim. She meant it right up until the point when Jimmy grabbed her arm as she pulled it past him. She dropped the plate. His grip so tight her hand instantly felt tingly and swollen.

"You might not give a damn about yourself, sweetheart, but right now there's four people, that I can think of, you do give a damn about".

Susan's heart flickered for a moment, warming slightly at the thought of the people she loved. How could she have forgotten them? How could she have placed her own needs above theirs? Yet she was the only one he was treating like this wasn't he?

She imagined the children playing in their room with their father and grandfather looking on, while she was alone and un-thought of. *Were* they trying to rescue *her*? Were they even thinking of her?

She felt as though someone was tearing her heart apart like an unwanted letter. Every awful feeling churned in her chest. Her brain was dizzy and drained. She could not even keep a simple thought in her head, instead hundreds, some irrelevant, flirted around her mind, colliding and exploding, causing a cacophony of confusion until finally she felt her body go limp and her vision go black.

Chapter Five

Footsteps, light, white shadows and disjointed noises. Susan woke with a start. She was alone, in her bedroom. Yet this time she knew she hadn't been dreaming. The back of her head felt bruised. She must have landed on it as she fainted. It was causing a dull ache behind her eyes and along her brow. The cut on her neck stung and also felt a little bruised. When she ran her finger over it she found a rough raised line.

She desperately needed the toilet and took this rare opportunity to use her en-suite without the off-putting surveillance she had grown to expect. After she had used the lavatory she considered showering but decided in the circumstances she should probably find out where Jimmy was before endeavouring to enjoy these simple luxuries she had once taken for granted.

The thought dawned on Susan that perhaps he had finally gone, she didn't know how long she had been unconscious, it could have been days. He could be a hundred miles away by now.

The only way to find out was to investigate.

She quietly looked around the room but found nothing, after this she headed for the door. She began pushing it open but the door slid only a few inches before being stopped, with a dull thud, by something soft. Susan jumped back.

It was a body!

Through the crack of the open door she made out a mass of thick brown curls. It must have been Jimmy's body lain outside the door. But why? Was he dead? Her heart leapt and fell simultaneously. If he was dead she was free, but too she was trapped. What would she say to explain the terrible events during her imprisonment? Would she be accused of killing him, or harbouring him?

She pushed the door again, harder, in an attempt to move the body enough to squeeze through the door. As the door thudded into Jimmy's body he stirred, again Susan's heart shuddered almost to a complete stand still.

"Hey!" he yelled with sleep infused gruffness, "Where do you think you're going?"

He rose uncoordinatedly as he spoke and, now completely upright, pulled the door from Susan's grip causing her to be slightly off balance.

"I..." she tried, but found that her throat was too dry to form the words properly.

Jimmy pushed her back into the bedroom with such force she fell back onto the bed. He slammed the door roughly behind him as he entered the room.

"You think I would leave you unguarded while I slept? You must think I'm stupid. You're more trouble than the rest of the family put together! Get this into your head, this is *my* house now, you *will* obey my rules and you'll stay where I put you or I will bring that pretty girl of yours in here and start slicing her up".

Susan, although she knew he was violent, was shocked by his words. He had always seemed to be aggressive to adults but she was sure he had been good to the children, so far.

Jimmy saw her shock.

"Don't believe me? Just try me!"

Susan didn't dare say a word or move. She didn't want to test him. If he were serious she would never forgive herself if he hurt someone because she had angered him, even if it wasn't Claire. She would hate to cause him to hurt Mrs Byron or anyone.

Jimmy winked, knowingly, the sickening smile curling half his lip.

"Glad we've reached an understanding".

He turned away and began to leave, before turning around with a frown on his face.

"I didn't kill that woman you know".

Susan frowned, confused, but Jimmy simply continued.

"The woman in the bank. I didn't shoot her. I didn't even have a gun. It was the guy I was doing the job with".

Susan realised he was talking about the murder he was imprisoned for committing.

"It's none of my business" Susan told him, hoping this was the right answer.

"Yes it is!" Jimmy yelled aggressively, causing Susan to jump with shock so violently she had to hold herself steady for a moment else fall off the bed. "All the people who've heard those bullshit lies should know the truth. I didn't kill that woman. I was only in the bank because I was desperate.

He sat on the bed beside Susan, leaning forward and looking down at his hands that he held entwined between his knees. My wife had got us in debt because of a smack habit. We were going to lose the house, and my kid was in danger. I had to get that money".

Susan was still confused by Jimmy's sudden change of attitude and need to explain.

"You don't have to tell me all this".

She barely finished her sentence before he had rounded on her. He was practically on top of her on the bed, his arms either side of her so she was trapped.

"Yes I do! You're not listening".

He was somehow more erratic and frightening than ever.

"I won't get a chance to tell everyone the truth, except you. I need someone to understand!"

A cloud lifted from Susan's mind. That's why he had kept so close to her. He must have realised she was the most likely person, from the family, to listen to him and pass on his version of events. Perhaps he wanted to clear his name, or maybe it was for his child. No wonder he had been good with Claire and Tom. He was a father. Susan had never imagined he had a wife or child. He did not seem the sort of person who would have a wedding day or stay up all night to feed a baby.

Did this sudden change mean that Jimmy was planning to leave soon? It definitely meant he intended to leave her alive.

With a sense of relief, "Alright" she ventured, hoping her co-operation would make him move off of her again, as the feel of his hot, rancid breath was causing a moist patch of rank condensation on her cheek.

Jimmy did move, he walked over to the window and looked out as he spoke.

"It all started going wrong about thirteen years ago, when my daughter was born." He looked at Susan with such intensity and imploring she was taken aback momentarily "It wasn't her fault! My little Molly never did anything to anyone!" With his point made his gaze flowed back to the window and his tone eased again. "Just before Moll was born my wife, Liz, got that post-natal depression that some women have. The pregnancy had been awful and the birth was worse. When Moll came out, she looked all weird. The doctors told us she had Down's syndrome. She was so tiny it broke my heart, and Liz just couldn't get her head round it. She just seemed to get more and more down.

"Moll was perfect. She was just a baby. She was eating right, growing perfect. I didn't even notice she was any different from any other kid after a bit, but Liz wouldn't touch her. Blamed herself. The doctor said there was nothing she did to make our little girl that way but she wouldn't listen. Just kept getting more and more distant until eventually she began to go missing for a couple of days at a time. I was worried sick, but she wouldn't talk to me and whenever I tried it just caused an argument, which made Moll upset. It got so we couldn't speak a civil word to each other. Then Liz vanished for above a week. Left me to try and figure out how to raise a downs baby and work at the same time. I couldn't do it. I had to think of Moll and my work didn't understand. They ended up letting me go and I had to live off thin air and savings.

"I noticed money was missing from our bank account. Quite a lot. We had been saving a deposit for a house, I didn't want to touch that money, but it got till I had no choice. I figured I could fall back on it until we got our shit back together, but when I checked the account there was nothing there. I had to question Liz about it. I needed to know where it had gone.

"I managed to get in touch with her through her parents; she was living in a dodgy squat with some pretty scary people. I didn't like it, I wanted my wife back, but she wasn't the same person, and all I could do now was think about my baby. She was nearly three by this point, and so bright!

"Turned out Liz had got onto smack and had spent all our savings on her habit.

"I found out she owed this guy a heap of money we couldn't repay. He was going to get nasty; he'd already smacked Liz about a bit. I think that's why she hadn't dared to come home. When I found her she was all beat up and looked a real mess. I would have kicked off and probably killed the guy if I had the chance to lay my hands on him" Again Jimmy turned to Susan with an intense look on his face "I'll admit that too. I would have killed that guy. But he deserved it Susan. He was killing people and wrecking other people's lives. He was a fucking scum bag and I would have been doing the world a favour!" Again he turned back to the window, but he still spoke tensely, as though it was taking every muscle to stop himself from smashing something in anger.

"So I was fucked. No job, no money, no wife and the most beautiful little girl who needed to be raised right. I didn't know what to do. I was so lost. I began to wish I was Liz. I actually wished I had been the one who had taken the easy route and left it all behind. How nuts is that? I was jealous of a skag head.

"I was so damn desperate that when I overheard this guy I knew, Jimmie, saying he had a plan to rob a bank I couldn't resist hearing him out. It really sounded like it'd work I thought I had to give it a chance. He said it wouldn't hurt anyone, like a house robbery would, so I decided to do it with him. I was desperate for the money I would have pretty much done anything.

"We planned everything to the last detail. It was going to be quick and clean and we would walk out of there with enough money keep us in the good life for years. We even figured out how to launder the money so no one would ever suspect a thing. It was perfect. It sounds so ridiculous now, but I was excited. I convinced myself that it was the only way and that everything would be okay.

"It all went to plan. We got into the bank without a hitch. We got the money without any cops being alerted and noon was being any trouble. Everyone just handed it over smooth. It was like clockwork. I hate to admit it but it was a real buzz. I started to feel like I could do anything. I guess Jimmie felt the same way too because as we were leaving he started acting like he was crazy. He started firing his gun off at the ceiling. He didn't mean to but he stumbled. Lost his footing while he was still shooting and ended up hitting this pregnant woman right through her eye. It was all kinds of fucked up! People were screaming. Everything was just a mass of gore and noise.

"I was so shocked I didn't know what to do. All I could think was to run. I grabbed Jimmie and we bolted. I don't know how, the cashier must have had a secret alarm but the cops were already outside. We didn't even have time to think about getting away. We were surrounded. I reckon even if we hadn't harmed anyone we would have still been caught. I think the cops must have been there as soon as we polled up.

"If we had just done the robbery we'd have been out by now, and I wouldn't have missed so much of Moll's life. Because that bird got killed the sentence was strict. They didn't even give me a chance to say I didn't shoot her. They threw the book at us both and we went down the same. We got a life sentence."

He continued looking intently out of the window. Susan's mind was whirling with questions. Unsure of whether she dare ask any of them. She too stared out of the window for a long moment before she finally plucked up courage to speak. After all, he did seem to want to confess all.

"What about the man you stabbed in prison?"

Jimmy visibly stiffened. It took a long moment for him to speak, and then it was through stiff, unwilling lips.

"He was a rapist. He got sent down for it and wasn't ashamed. He didn't let the lack of women inside stop him either. He thought he could mess with me. Cornered and overpowered me in the showers. He could have managed it as well if the pigs hadn't caught him first. Only time the bastards weren't trying to screw me over themselves".

For the first time in his confessions he looked at her briefly, as though he was trying to judge her reactions. She felt as though he was pausing for her to speak.

"If the prison guards stopped him, why'd you stab him?"

Jimmy flinched, his face tensed, he looked like a rabbit caught in the headlights. He turned back to the window.

"I couldn't let him get away with it. He wasn't getting punished in that place. He was running it, bossing everyone about. He'd been winding me up since he came in. Bragging, threatening. I just did enough to teach him a lesson".

He looked at her again, his eyes wide and fixed upon her face. Lips tight.

"I'm not a bad bloke Susan." She flinched, it was the first time he'd used her name. "But ..." he added unpleasantly "I don't take any crap".

And Susan knew he meant it.

"What about that police officer? The one you stabbed when you escaped".

"Him!" Jimmy turned and moved towards the bed, sweepingly.

"He deserved it".

Susan was shocked by this turn, but couldn't resist asking more questions. She felt like a magician slowly pulling handkerchiefs of information from Jimmy's sleeves.

"Why?"

Jimmy looked annoyed, but not at her. The thought of the police officer was infuriating him. It was as if he couldn't stop himself from talking.

"He was talking bad about my girl. He said she was a whore. She's only twelve. He was saying Liz got in with a dealer. He was smacking them both about. This cop was laughing, teasing me all the way as they were taking me to court 'cos I stabbed that scumbag in jail and all the way he wouldn't shut up and he just kept on and on.

"He kept talking about my Moll. He said she had become a whore to pay her way without parents. He said she was a smack head too. Said he'd been with her. Said a load of shit a about her. It was all bull! She's a good girl. She doesn't have it in her to do that kind of thing. She's sweet, and beautiful. Better than Liz and me, better than we deserve. How would you feel if they'd said that about your little girl?"

He paused briefly for a moment, staring intently at Susan's face, trying to judge her reactions at the thought of Claire being molested. She knew he was unsatisfied by her lack of horror, but he had threatened this every second since he had arrived.

Susan had simply raised an eyebrow and gave him a sarcastic look that she hoped emphasised to him what a hypocrite he was.

For a brief moment it felt as though he recognised a connection between the anguish he had felt at that time and the agony he was putting her through himself at this very moment.

But as quickly as the flicker of understanding had twinkled in his eyes it disappeared again and Jimmy continued as though nothing at all had happened.

"He wound me up so much, I flipped. May be Moll was in trouble, getting hurt. I was getting close to home. I had to find out how my baby girl was. That guy I sliced in the nick deserved it. I'd have got off in court, I was sure, but I couldn't risk it. As it was I'd still got a life sentence to serve. I couldn't leave her any longer. She was in danger.

"The fact that he got in my way wasn't my fault, he shouldn't have been such a dick"

"Jimmy, you can't just stab people because they upset you".

Susan couldn't believe she had said something so patronising, but her motherly instinct had chimed in. Both Claire and Tom had behaved similarly when toddlers. They used to kick or hit out when they didn't get their way. Jimmy was so like a child it would almost be sweet if he were not trying to kill people.

"Prison", Jimmy mumbled. "It's dog-eat-dog. I thought I was in for life. I had to change and become like this to survive".

Susan didn't need to imagine how he felt, the last few days had shown her. She had changed and adapted in order to survive. Would she be able to kill him if she needed? She would want to if anything happened to her babies. Perhaps they weren't so different, even though she didn't understand how he could justify cutting someone just because they'd made him angry.

"So what are you going to do now?" she asked, almost hoping she could help.

"Do you have a plan?" If he did and she helped she could get him out of her life quickly, because there was no one else who was going to help her.

A tide of confusion momentarily flushed across Jimmy's face.

"Are you taking the piss?" he asked.

Susan wasn't. She was no longer scared of him or afraid at all. She just wanted to get him out of her home and out of her life forever.

"No! I'm serious. Just tell me what I can do and leave my family safe".

Jimmy looked as if he didn't understand. As if no one had ever offered him any help before. Taking Susan by surprise, a genuine smile of happiness appeared on his face. It turned him from the cruel faced invader she had become used to, into a handsome man she wished she knew in different circumstances. For a moment Susan thought she could see the soft glint of a tear in Jimmy's left eye, but before she had a chance to find out he suddenly spoke.

"Do you want a shower?"

Jimmy's question and shifting attitudes were surprising Susan but she was happy to take advantage of his accommodating attitude.

"Yes I do," she said softly.

Jimmy simply pointed towards the en suite before saying

"You can even shut the door, it's not like you can escape". He smiled again.

Susan smiled in return as she got up from the bed and went into the en suite. She closed the door thankfully. The privacy Jimmy was allowing her was much appreciated, but just to feel extra secure she sneakily slid the lock across. She didn't want Jimmy to hear in case he thought she didn't trust him. If he did hear it lock he didn't bother because Susan undressed without disturbance. She turned on the shower. Even before the water ran warm it felt heavenly against her testing hand.

Once it was warm enough Susan ventured in. The water felt beautiful as it ran down her body. She simply stood, unmoving for some time, simply enjoying the cleansing pleasure.

She began by washing her hair. It had become very unpleasant and greasy on her head over her days of captivity. The shampoo felt silky on her scalp and the flowery smell emitted by the tiny popping bubbles made her realise just how dirty she had become. She washed the rest of her body quickly and even shaved her legs, as they had become prickly and uncomfortable. Again she stood under the flow of warm water just to enjoy its caressing sensation.

She stepped out of the shower feeling completely new. She wrapped a fresh fluffy towel around her body and another around her hair. She looked at herself in the mirror over the sink. Though it had only been a few days locked in her house she had visibly lost some weight. She was used to three square home cooked meals a day. She had been fortunate to get two small meals as it was. Her eyes were slightly sunken in, puffy and a little dark around the dips in her nose. She dried her face without taking her eyes off of the reflection.

Her teeth felt fuzzy and tongue tasted tangy and unpleasant. She wasn't sure if Jimmy had intended her to brush her teeth while she was washing, but she felt she had to. She ran the water and dipped he brush underneath. The cold of the brush and the fresh minty burst of toothpaste in her mouth gave her a sudden jolt of alertness. She gave her teeth a good scrub and rinsed out her mouth.

She looked back to her clothes. She felt so fresh and nice that she didn't want to wear them again, but she didn't want to be in the same room as Jimmy wearing only a towel.

She sat on the toilet for a moment. She just wanted a few quiet minutes to enjoy her freshness before opening the door and being back in a house being run by an escaped convict. She shut her eyes for a moment.

Susan jolted at the sound of a knock at the door. She opened her eyes and realised she had nodded off. She didn't know how long for but her skin was dry and her hair almost was.

"Susan" Jimmy sounded concerned, "Susan, Are you alright?"

"Yes. Yes, I'm sorry, I must have fallen asleep".

The handle on the door lifted up. Jimmy must have let go of it.

"Hurry up. I need you to do something".

Without thinking it through Susan went out into her room. Now that she was fresh she noticed a musty smell in her room, it must have been caused by their two unclean bodies stuck in it for days.

Jimmy looked at her hungrily and she remembered she was only wearing a towel. She became scared immediately as she felt incredibly exposed. Jimmy licked his bottom lip like he had several times before and Susan felt sure he was going to rape her. Had he included that in the things he was going to make her do?

"Get dressed"

He threw some clean clothes onto the bed and went out of the room without another word. He shut the door behind him and Susan knew he remained outside as no footsteps padded down the stairs.

She dressed slowly, again pleased for the privacy and trying to prolong it. Jimmy had picked out more suitable clothing this time. A little Tee shirt, jumper and jeans and Susan wondered if it was just a coincidence or had he planned the outfit, as it looked quite nice as she glanced in the mirror.

"I'm dressed" she called and Jimmy returned.

"Look out the window".

She did and saw a different sight.

Chapter Six

The thick snow that had previously blanketed the entire landscape now had a thick black scar leading right to the horizon.

"The road" she whispered. An uncontrollable smile curled the corners of Susan's lips. Finally she wasn't so secluded. Finally Jimmy could leave. She tried to stifle a manic giggle of excitement as she looked at him.

"What now?"

Jimmy, without a word, walked to the door. He turned and beckoned her to follow. She shadowed him down the stairs and into the kitchen. The smell of rotting food was now intense. It made Susan's nostrils sting to inhale. It was going to take a long time to wash the terrible stink out of her life.

Jimmy motioned towards the fridge.

"Foods off, and there's no more cereals. We need to get supplies".

He moved over to the kitchen window and looked out.

"I can't go. I'll be seen. You have to go or we all starve".

Susan felt elated at the thought of leaving her confinement. Sheer joy swept over her. She could go to the police or let someone know what was happening. She was smiling, unable to stop, until Jimmy continued:

"I've made a list of things I want. For every thing missing from the list, you pick a family member and I will slice them apart when you get back. For every five minutes you're late back, I'll pick a family member, from youngest to oldest and slice them apart".

Susan's heart sank. The thought of being on the outside thrilled her, but the knowledge that she had a near impossible mission left a heavy weight in her chest. She half wanted to refuse Jimmy's offer but could tell from his face that she had no choice.

"What do you want me to fetch?" she asked tentatively, knowing if lime and spades were on the list she would definitely take her chances and starve. Jimmy picked up a pre prepared list from the kitchen counter. It had around twenty items, all mundane and probably available within a couple of shops. She looked up from the list and into Jimmy's face.

"How long do I have?"

Jimmy looked at the clock over the door. He raised his eyes and mouthed something before flicking his eyes back down to her.

"An hour".

Susan felt her jaw drop in surprise.

"An hour?" she questioned, feeling shocked and scared. That was surely impossible, she must have misunderstood.

"Yes! An hour" he said irritably.

"But that's impossible Jimmy".

He must have been confused by the enormity of the task he was setting her.

"You said ..." he began, as slowly as if he was talking to an insolent child, "that it would take ten minutes to get in to town. Ten minutes back that leaves you forty minutes to do the shopping. I'm being very generous with the time".

"It takes ten minutes to get to the outskirts of the town on a normal day" she argued. "With the snow it could take forever, especially if I get stuck behind a plough".

She was getting frustrated and desperate.

"Then when I get to town I've got to park, then get everything. And what if there's a big queue at the check out?"

She felt a big lump in her throat as her words began to choke her as she tried to hold back tears.

"I can't do it in an hour, please, I need more time".

Jimmy looked at her down his nose as if he was disgusted at her begging. Then his eyes twitched and his expression changed slightly.

"An hour and a half. But that's all you're getting. And if I so much as suspect the police are on their way, I'll kill everyone without a second thought" he added nastily.

Susan knew arguing was futile. The look on his face was determined and definite.

"When do I go?"

Jimmy went round the corner into the pantry. Susan heard some tumbling before he emerged with her coat.

"Now" he said as he thrust it towards her. She began to put it on, as she did she got a strong smell, which caught in her throat and almost made her gag. Jimmy looked shocked as she tried to hold down the rising feeling of sickness.

"What?" he asked harshly.

"My coat" she said feeling nauseous "it stinks"

Her nose was getting used to the smell slightly and her stomach began to settle.

"It must have got damp when you went out to dig the snow" he said, as though she should have known this.

She wouldn't have usually cleared the path, but if she had she wouldn't have worn this fleecy coat. It must have become slightly mouldy hung in up the pantry. Also, she thought, it was likely the unpleasant odours of the rotting food had knitted themselves into the fibres of the material.

"I need my car keys," she informed Jimmy who rolled his eyes.

"Well get them then" he said, making Susan feel annoyed.

She made her way towards the pantry.

"Where are you going?" he asked, practically throwing himself in front of her path.

Susan frowned. She couldn't understand this man, not matter how hard she tried. Every time she thought she was getting used to his nuances he would rapidly change completely. It was almost as if he had two conflicting personalities in perpetual battle.

"My keys are in my bag" Susan informed him. "The bag is in the pantry".

She felt tired and annoyed. She couldn't stand this continual struggle to keep on his, ever changing, good side.

"I'll get it. You stay here".

Susan wanted to swear and stamp her feet in frustration. He was slowly driving her to distraction. Did he honestly expect her to follow his differing ideas of how she should behave?

Jimmy fumbled about in the pantry causing Susan to wonder if he had found the light or was banging about in the dark. If she hadn't been so peeved she would have found it slightly amusing. Susan decided to proffer some assistance.

"It's a brown leather bag. It should be on the floor," she yelled.

There was another few load thumps and bashes before the sound of flesh hitting the tiled floor. Jimmy swore loudly.

"Are you alright Jimmy?"

"Yes" he shouted back. "Stay where you are".

He need not have bothered telling her. She had no intention of moving. She was, in fact, quite pleased he had fallen over. She felt a twinge of pleasure at the idea of him hurting himself.

After a few more moments of listening to Jimmy bang about and mutter barely audible profanities he returned, looking rather sweaty and harried.

"Here".

He thrust the bag towards her. Susan was tempted to say it was the wrong bag, just to tease him, but she knew this sad attempt at revenge would do nothing besides anger him.

She took the bag from his hand and went towards the kitchen door which was usually used as their main entrance so that the light coloured carpet in the hall didn't get muddied by the clumsy family, and cluttered with their jettisoned coats, shoes and bags. Before she managed to even reach the pantry, Jimmy grabbed her arm and spun her back into the room.

"Front door" he said as he began gently pushing her in front of him.

She couldn't care less at this stage and decided not to correct him by informing him they never used it. They reached the door, which Jimmy opened and stood hidden behind it. Before she managed to get all the way out of the door Jimmy spoke.

"Act natural. And be back by five thirty on the dot".

Susan went to the car as quickly as she could. Once inside she started it and began to back out of the front yard. She glanced at the clock. It was almost five minutes to four. She had an extra five minutes. Was it enough?

Then her eyes landed on the fuel gauge. She was running out of petrol. She always liked to keep the tank above half full in case of emergencies but, now there was one, the tank was below a quarter full. She didn't have time to worry about this now. She just had to hope it lasted until she returned home.

She drove as fast as she dared on the still slippery road. The plough had also gritted and the salty little pebbles crackled and flicked the side of the car as she drove. It was making Susan cringe. Mark was very particular about the condition of the car and she wondered if he would be mad that she wasn't driving more carefully. She was making fair time and she contemplated the idea that if she continued at this pace she may have enough time to inform someone of the murderer in her house. Her heart felt as though someone was wringing it out with their hands. She didn't think, even with spare time, she had the guts to do it. It sounded stupid even in her own mind, but the idea of anyone interfering terrified her. They could jeopardise the lives of everyone in the house, including her own.

With a heavy thumping heartbeat, which Susan could feel right into her fluttering stomach, she finally reached town. As she had got closer the snow had lessened until here there was hardly any. Of course the town was so much lower than her house. Some small drifts of untrodden snow close to walls remained, but mainly just cold damp pavements and slush. Even the icicles on buildings seemed to be beginning to gradually melt away.

She decided that if she could get everything in one shop she would have enough time to call the police.

She managed to get a parking space near the door of the local hypermarket. It had taken her almost fifteen minutes but if she could dash round and get everything quickly; she would have enough time to get some help. She got out of the car and tried to walk as fast as possible without raising suspicion.

She picked up a basket and hurried around, grabbing items off the shelves and dropping them into the basket, still trying to rush but remain as unnoticed as possible.

She felt as though she was burning up. The harsh, thudding pulse that she could feel from her toes to her fingertips seemingly pumped all her blood into her face. Her eyes began to feel warm, her lids heavy and her legs weak. She knew if she didn't calm herself soon she would faint, and never have a chance to get home in time.

She thrust the penultimate item from the list into her basket. Only crisps remained on the list. She knew they would be here, and she hurried to the aisle. The basket, now heavy, dug into her tired arm. She reached the crisps aisle and glanced at her watch. It had taken her well below fifteen minutes to get the shopping. She darted down between rows of crisps and sweets. It had always stressed her out before, but in comparison to this she longed for those little annoyances. She grabbed the bag of crisps from the shelf and headed to the tills.

Although she knew she had bustled past several slow moving shoppers, with her mind concentrating so profusely, she hadn't realised quite how busy the shop was. It was only now that she had to join an incredibly long till queue that she saw the volume of people.

As she stood there, mentally urging the slow moving till operator. She wondered about the reason for this increased amount of business. Had she missed a few days whilst unconscious? Had she been imprisoned for longer than three days? It should be Tuesday afternoon. It shouldn't be this busy on an early afternoon mid week. Why weren't people at work?

The queue inched forward before a woman Susan knew from Tom's school attached herself to it.

"Hello Suzie" she said cheerfully.

Susan couldn't really stand Melissa Drury, but she put up with her for the sake of Tom who was friends with her son Hugo. She also hated being called Suzie and so in return, in secret, she and Mark referred to Melissa as Molasses. After all she was sweet and sickly.

"Hi Mel".

Melissa seemed positively jubilant. It made Susan feel sick. How dare she feel so happy while she was going through hell?

"I bet you're loving the kids being home".

Susan frowned. "How do you know they're home?"

Melissa giggled as she patted Susan patronisingly on her arm.

"You make me laugh Suzie". She didn't answer Susan's question, instead she seemed distracted by her own mind.

"Terrifying though isn't it?" she said, not giving Susan time to answer. "Can you imagine how frightening it would be if you spotted him?"

Her face and hands moved animatedly as the queue inched forward again.

"I don't dare leave the house when it starts getting darker".

Making Susan jump, the woman before her in the queue chimed up. She was elderly and Susan knew her as the grandmother of another child from the school.

"I've been sleeping with a knife under my pillow" she said as though she should be rewarded. "And even if the school wasn't closed, I bloody well wouldn't be sending in our Joe" she added matter-of-factly.

Melissa began to speak back to her.

"I know exactly what you mean. My two think I'm really cruel because I won't even let them play on the garden unless my Geoff's out there with them".

Susan realised they must have been talking of Jimmy. Should she say something? If she did would they be able to help? Would they even believe her?

She stood between the two gossiping women feeling like a complete outsider. She was no longer one of them. She was never going to quite fit in again because she was changed forever. She was alone with her experience, unpleasantly unique. More desperately than ever before, Susan craved the company of her family, possibly the only people who could ever understand, and yet still not quite.

Then out of the shadows of despair a flickering light of hope began to grow.

"... door to door police checks..." Melissa was saying. "They came to ours yesterday".

Susan remembered the newsreader mentioning this, but she had been side tracked and had forgotten.

The grandmother was now speaking as the flickering light of hope began to flame into a warming beacon.

"They've been to ours too. Have they been to yours dear?" she asked Susan.

"No" she said, almost ready to erupt. "They will soon I expect".

Melissa laughed. "Probably today" she said smiling. "They were heading that way".

Addressing the old lady she said, "Suzie lives up at Pottery Cottage, near old Mrs Byron".

The old lady giggled. "Less of the old, young lady. I went to school with Dora Byron".

Susan's mind faded out slightly. What if the police arrived now? What if they were finding him now? Her heart fluttered, but she knew that Jimmy would be too smart to just answer the door. He'd either ignore it or send Mark to answer it. Susan was about to ask Melissa what the door-to-door checks involved. Did they come in and have a look around? The old lady intruded into Susan's thoughts. Her smile faded a little to be replaced by a contemplative look.

"They won't be heading up there yet. Not since there was that sighting up near the moors".

"What?" asked Susan, the words bursting from her lips like a bullet from a gun.

The old lady continued, evidently not noticing Susan's abrupt reaction.

"I know. As if someone could survive up there in this weather. They have to follow all the leads though don't they? I mean, he could be there and they'd feel pretty awful if they'd ignored it. Mind you, if all these sightings are genuine he's getting about a bit. In my opinion he's miles away. That or he's charmed some stupid girl into hiding him".

Susan felt sick to the pit of her stomach. Stupid girl? Was that what people would think of her? She couldn't stop the words tumbling out of her mouth. She was miles away in a dazed world of her own.

"He could be holding someone hostage. He could be terrorising some poor family".

Both women became sombre, faces clouding over seriously. Susan had never seen Melissa this way.

"We know Suzie," she said coldly. "It's scary but we've got to play it down or we'd be terrified". Melissa's eyes began to glaze and her cheeks reddened.

"You're out of it up there out of town. Everyone's terrified down here; it's all anyone talks about. The kids are crying themselves to sleep and we're on tenterhooks. I don't dare have any of my curtains open when it starts getting dark".

The queue had moved down and the old lady was being served. Susan realised that she wasn't the only prisoner in town. As she looked at the faces of the other shoppers she saw they all wore tired and worried expressions. They held their children tightly and hurried about their business. It felt as though she had a duty to protect her friends. She couldn't tell Melissa that Jimmy was not only local but in her house. She would have to control the situation herself, a vigilante. A strange strength welled in her.

She had lived the nightmare that was haunting all these people and she had survived. She was strong enough to handle anything. She could live through this, she knew she could.

The cashier began swooping Susan's things through, causing her to snap back to the moment. She checked her watch. She had been in the check out queue for just over ten minutes. She was running out of time. She only had an hour to go to the authorities and get home.

Usually Susan would have sorted her shopping into carefully designated bags, but right now she didn't care. She slammed anything anyhow, bid a brief farewell to Melissa and bolted to the exit, focused only on making her way to the police station.

A hand stopped her.

Susan, filled with a heavy sense of foreboding, followed her eyes up the thin, dark arm and into the sunken grey eyes and leathery features.

"Mrs Byron!"

"Hello dear. I thought it was you. You look ever so poorly love. Are you alright?"

Susan was desperate to get away and was only just listening.

"Yes".

"Oh", said Mrs Byron, taken aback by the abruptness with which Susan had answered. Now feeling curious she continued.

"Is it the kids? Still off it? I think you may have caught whatever it is".

Susan just nodded. She knew she was being rude but couldn't concentrate on anything but getting to the police station. Although she loved Mrs Byron she was in the way of her. If she didn't shut up Susan was getting so desperate she would simply have to knock her out of the way.

"It must be bad, flu may be. It's not very often your Tom doesn't play out; especially when there's snow on the ground, bless him. Your Claire's getting big now, isn't she?" Mrs Byron didn't pause for an answer, just for a breath. "How's Jack? It's scary when you get older. The next little cough could knock you off your feet".

Susan wasn't taking in anything her neighbour was saying, she just nodded and smiled, wishing beyond hope that she would let her go. The seconds were ticking by; she could practically see them, like grains of sand tumbling clumsily though an hourglass.

On several occasions Susan attempted to leave the conversation and escape to the police but she didn't want to hurt Mrs Byron's feelings or cause her to intrude. If she began interfering, as Mrs Byron tended to do, she would be a liability, a danger to herself and everyone in Susan's house.

Finally Mrs Byron's conversation slowed to a halt.

"Well I've kept you long enough, duck. Get yourself off home and have a nice long, relaxing bath".

Determined to get away from the conversation immediately Susan mumbled a quick attempt at a pleasant goodbye and she bolted out of the door, almost walking into a sandwich board.

She looked at her watch again. Mrs Byron had held her back another ten minutes. She now had only three quarters of an hour to get to the police and to get home.

She headed off into the centre of town before she realised she didn't have a clue where the police station was. With all the anxiety and excitement she hadn't even realised she didn't know the location of the police station. It hadn't even crossed her mind.

She felt as though she was about to lose all the strength in her muscles. How was she going to find the police station without drawing unwanted attention to herself?

She looked around, desperately searching for something that might point out the way, but she was beginning to feel dazed. Her eyes were beginning to lose focus and again she felt sure she would faint. She stood and leaned against a wall. It was as though she was never destined to find a way out of the situation. She couldn't do anything right. Forty-five minutes wouldn't give her enough time to get across town if she needed to. She guessed the station would be somewhere near to the town hall but she wouldn't get there in time.

Every single minute since Jimmy had entered the house had stretched out so it felt as though her life before him had never really existed, yet this hour and half without him had whipped past as though it was only seconds.

There was nothing she could do, beyond voluntarily get back into her car and drive herself back into the cage Jimmy had created.

The part of her brain that controlled her body gave up and she slid down the wall and onto the floor. Familiar despairing tears coursed down her face. She was totally alone, unprotected and completely lost.

She felt as though there was a hand on her chest was holding her back. She would have done almost anything to stay here, curled up in a pathetic heap, but safe. The only thing she wouldn't give up was the only thing he had. Her family were worth more than every penny she had ever earned, her home, her car and every possession. They were worth more than her own life because she would rather be dead than live without them.

The thought of how much they needed her to be strong, gripped Susan. They were in danger and she couldn't abandon them. The thought of Jimmy flinging Claire around, like he did when he first came to the house gave her the energy to stand back up. She walked quickly back to the car and got inside. She was close to giving up again, as her muscles slackened when she sat, but she quickly pulled herself together and carried on.

Every slight movement she had to make took masses of strength and determination. The effort needed simply to breathe expended more energy than she ever knew she could muster.

As she started the car her eyes fixed on the orange light indicating she was out of fuel. Although she had enough time to go straight home she doubted she had enough time to go and fill up the car with petrol. She knew her purse was close to empty so she couldn't afford to fill up without first nipping to a bank. She just had to hope the petrol remaining would be enough to get her home; else the price would be the lives of her family. How awful to be stranded at the side of the road, so close, while that mad man viciously hacked away at her life. She shuddered, more hot tears pulled from her swelling eyes.

The drive home seemed to last for hours. The sky was turning dusky and grey, adding to Susan's despairing feelings. She hated this time of day. It always depressed her. She kept flicking her eyes to the clock, but mere minutes were plodding past. She wondered if she would have had time to find the police station and get help, but she knew in her heart she wouldn't.

A cold ache swelled behind her breast, filling her chest with an agonising sick excitement. It pulled her forwards but intensified with every mile she drew closer to home. As the feeling boiled hotter the further she drove, it pushed up an acid lump in her throat until she felt sure she would vomit.

Again more and more tears welled in her eyes and rolled down her already soaked cheeks. She didn't care, nor did she care about the cold mucous that her crying had caused to form in her nose or the ruddiness in her face.

She was aware of the cars speed, and longed to slam her foot down, to get there faster, but knew if she did she would surely get pulled over. The thought crossed her mind that this would mean she could talk to the police, but she didn't dare cross Jimmy, and even if she did she didn't pass any police.

Her eyes continually flicked to the orange light and the fuel gauge needle sinking ever lower causing the pounding overpowering tension she felt to grow in her already aching chest.

With every mile she travelled closer to home, the lure of returning to town and freedom seemed harder to resist. She regretted the thought instantly, but she couldn't help toying with the idea of just leaving it all behind and leaving them all to deal with Jimmy themselves.

This awful thought circling her exhausted brain only served to make her body feel more out of control and aggravating. She felt as though she were two people conflicting with each other and at war. Was she going insane? She would have to be to even entertain leaving her family to die.

She began to feel less flustered and more angry. Furious in fact. Furious with herself for wanting to be selfish, furious at Jimmy for doing this to them, furious with Mark for letting him in and furious at the world for not helping.

Susan was within running distance of the house and her family's safety, even though the orange fuel light still taunted her she knew she could make it home in time, even if she had to get out and run the last few yards. She thumped the glass window beside her with frustration as she turned onto the slippery trail Jimmy had made her dig.

Once she had released this small twitch of aggression she felt as though she was overloaded with anger. She pulled up sharply and yanked on the brake, got out of the car, slammed the door and fell on her knees, screaming and punching the piled snow at the side of the path.

Then she saw it in the corner of her eye. She looked up along the bright, untainted snow through the open gate in the garden fence. An igloo! Susan wouldn't have believed she could feel more anger than she had but now she was practically drunk with an insane fury beyond her control. While she had been living a nightmare, lying to her friends and worrying about everyone's safety they had been here, playing in the snow. Did they even care about her at all? They obviously hadn't suffered like she had. They were just living a different lifestyle, while she was being practically tortured.

Susan went into the garden. She couldn't bring herself to look at the stupid igloo. She let herself into the kitchen and dropped her bags onto the floor before yelling

"I'm home".

Jimmy appeared from the dining room looking surprised and sweaty.

"You're early," he said, almost irritably, "and I told you to use the main door".

Susan had forgotten.

"Sorry". She proffered the shopping bags to him. "I got everything you wanted though".

Jimmy snatched the bags and began rummaging through them. He lined up all the tins, packets and boxes and examined them for a moment.

"Okay". He was calmer now. "Did you speak to anyone?"

Susan felt she had to lie. After all he would never believe her if she said she had spoken to several friends but kept him a secret.

"Not a soul". She looked out of the kitchen window. "You guys have been playing outside I see. Has everyone been out there while I've been gone?"

A teasing smile crept across Jimmy's face as he answered.

"Oh yes. I thought it would do everyone good to get out into the fresh air".

Susan, anger ebbing slightly, took off her coat and handed it to Jimmy who looked at her blankly.

"What?" he asked.

"I thought you would want to put it in the pantry yourself"

Jimmy frowned again. "You thought wrong. Do it yourself"

Susan was stunned. He had been so insistent she wasn't to go into the pantry. Why had he changed his mind suddenly? She went to it and opened the door, a stale rotting smell issued from it that almost knocked Susan backwards. Holding her breath she looked around the small space. It had been completely ransacked. Jars were smashed and strewn around, with other food debris just anyhow over the floor. The coats, usually hung up neatly, were scattered amongst the mouldy food. No wonder her coat had reeked so badly earlier.

Feeling stupid for doing so, she hung her coat on one of the now empty hooks and her bag on another. At which point she noticed that the broom was missing. A thought occurred to her. Jimmy must have torn the pantry apart to remove any potential weapons. That must have been why, until now, he wouldn't let in, in case she came out wielding an axe.

Why hadn't she thought of it before? There was an axe in one of the small outbuildings. Mark used it to chop firewood. How could she have been so stupid? She could have grabbed the axe while she had been out just now. She could have taken Jimmy by surprise, coming back early or never even going at all. She cursed herself for being so narrow sighted. Why hadn't she spent the last hour and a half concocting a plan? Buying a knife? She shouldn't have bothered with the shopping at all. She should have spent that time finding a police officer and getting herself rescued. She swore under her breath. "Damn!"

She had been so scared her mind had thought of nothing but obeying Jimmy's stupid rules. She wasn't an idiot. She would have been yelling at the screen if she had just seen herself in a movie. She felt so mad, with herself, with her family and with Jimmy. Everything seemed to be conspiring against her. May be she even deserved this.

No!

Susan's clouded, foggy; questioning mind suddenly became clear and focused. She could still do something. She could still get the axe.

So far every night she had been either passed out or observed totally. If she could get Jimmy to leave her alone, even for twenty minutes, it might give her the chance to get outside and grab the axe. It would be no match against a gun but she hadn't seen that since the first night so maybe she had a slim chance. All she had to think of now was how to get him to leave her alone.

She went back into the kitchen, where she could breathe properly again, even though the smell had lingered here as well. Thinking fast she asked:

"Shall I make tea again?" this caused Jimmy to eye her up and down as though looking for a hidden meaning.

"No! Go to your room".

Although the command was insulting and made her feel like a naughty child, Susan's heart filled with excitement. She had to walk out of the kitchen fairly quickly before she burst out laughing. She went through the hall and was making her way loudly upstairs, from where she intended to sneak straight back down, when Jimmy called her back. Her heart sank, but at least she was getting close. "Susan, get here now". Jimmy's voice sounded strange, panicky. "Susan!"

She rushed in to find him wide eyed and staring out of the window.

"Who did you speak to?" he yelled maniacally.

Susan's chest pounded.

"No one, I told you" she lied.

"Well who the fuck's that?"

He pointed out of the window to a set of headlights bobbing down the slippery lane off the main road. Susan thought. It wouldn't be Mrs Byron, she always caught the bus unless Mr Byron took her in his clapped out old red tractor, which was rare because Dora hated it. And those lights were neither the right size nor shape for a tractor.

"I don't know," she admitted.

After all it could have been anyone. Perhaps it was Mrs Byron's daughter visiting her, or even one of Susan and Mark's friends. The car turned onto Mrs Byron's drive.

"It must be her daughter" Susan informed, but as she spoke the security light flicked on and illuminated the car. As it passed the light rolled across the band of fluorescent yellow along the side of the car, and as it turned slightly to park, as clear as crystal Susan read, in bold navy letters "POLICE".

She felt as though she would throw up. Not for the first time she experienced that awful hope and simultaneous dread sensation. Potentially she was moments away from rescue, and yet a million things could go wrong.

"You called the pigs!" Jimmy virtually screamed. "You fucking bitch! I trusted you!"

He was pacing erratically and listing profanities to describe the situation. He seemed to physically swell as his rage intensified. He had turned in an instant into a huge terrifying being that occupied every inch of the world and Susan's soul. A creature of pure evil, barely human at all. So terrible was he that Susan froze on the spot filled with unrivalled fear.

"I didn't call the police, Jimmy. I got the shopping and came back. They're doing door to door checks," she said imploringly.

"You fucking liar. How do you expect me to believe that?"

Susan's mind raced for a moment.

"If I'd called them they would have come straight here wouldn't they?"

Jimmy's left eye twitched as he processed the thought. He visibly began to calm. The monster seeping back to its hiding place within this man.

"Yes", he said finally, eye still flickering. "Give me your keys", he yelled unexpectedly.

Without even considering disobeying Susan fetched her bag from the pantry, not daring to contemplate the fact that this nightmare could finally be coming to an end. She brought her bag out and began feeling around for her keys. She could tell Jimmy was becoming agitated but she genuinely couldn't put her hand on them.

"Stop stalling" Jimmy yelled as snatched her bag away, just as her finger brushed a cold metal key ring.

Jimmy began fishing around in her bag, searching for the keys. Evidently he was having as much difficulty finding them as she had. Susan felt a little embarrassed by the things Jimmy might find in her bag, like her tampons, but she mentally reprimanded herself for having such a trivial thought at such a crucial moment.

"They're not in here", he said gruffly, but he had grabbed them before he finished the sentence, and with a clanging jolt, pulled them out of the bag.

"What are you going to do?" Susan asked, bubbling with excitement and horror, knowing what his answer would be but needing confirmation nevertheless.

"I'm taking your car and getting as far away from here as I can".

Susan was so happily overwhelmed with joy she had to stop herself from screaming ecstatically. After all he wasn't gone yet. Although she knew he wouldn't kill her, she didn't want to tempt fate.

Then, like a flash of light, Susan's mind threw up an image. The fuel gauge. She had only just managed to get home on the fumes from the petrol left in the tank. Jimmy would be lucky to make it into town. There was no way he would get far. The police would easily catch him before he even got out of the county.

Susan had to practice extreme self-control as her entire body filled with near palpable joy. She could never remember feeling quite so happy and light, beyond the birth of her children. Her whole body tingled with near orgasmic pleasure. The excitement in her chest barely containable.

She was getting her life back, and although she would never be exactly the same, she was sure she would be able to enjoy her wonderful life to the full once she had her family back safe. In fact life would be so much richer. She would never again take anything for granted or over react at something irrelevant. She was alive, properly alive like never before, because she had tasted bitter death.

Jimmy threw Susan's bag onto the kitchen floor in a clattering heap, but she didn't care. He then ran to the back door. Susan felt literally sick with excitement. He was going to leave, he was actually going. But then, just as his hand rested on the door handle, he paused and looked back at her. His eyes, as they had done so many times before, flicked over her body. What had caused him to stop? Was he going to try and take her with him? Oh God, please just let him leave me alone, she prayed.

Jimmy sprung to the pantry door and yanked it open. He briefly disappeared inside and returned with some thick twine that Jack used to tie up his plants.

He jerked the twine taught between his hands and approached Susan. He was going to tie her up. If she hadn't known that the police were so close she would have been frightened, but she really didn't care. She had to practically stop herself from getting the chair for him to tie her too, but she knew if she showed too much eagerness he would think she had called the police.

He grabbed a tall chair from the breakfast bar. Susan barely used these as they were beautiful but uncomfortable. He faced it to the kitchen window and pushed her harshly onto it. He began to work the twine around the rungs on the chair and Susan's limbs. He pulled tightly and ran the twine quickly, causing painful burns on Susan's wrists. She was beginning to feel uncomfortable and the familiar dread began to soak into her bones once more. What if the police didn't come and find her. She could be stuck here for days?

Jimmy didn't stop tying her down until every bit of twine was used. There was no way she could have escaped. She could barely move at all. As a last act of cruelty Jimmy grabbed a wash cloth from beside the sink and rammed it into Susan's mouth. It stunk of stale water and tasted rank and dry in her mouth but she couldn't remove it as her hands were so securely tied beside her.

After taking one last look about the room Jimmy proceeded to bolt out of the back door with great haste, and with that Jimmy Bailey walked out of Susan's home as abruptly as he had entered it.

Susan sat in shock for a long time. She watched as her car lights came on and sped away down the slippery lane. She watched as the police cars headlights soon joined them in hot pursuit and she watched as Mr and Mrs Byron came out of their front door and looked over at her house with expressions of fear and shock.

She sat for so long that all the action had died away before she realised what had happened.

He was gone! He was actually out of their lives, their home. Except in photographs on the news and in the papers she would never have to see his foul face again.

Chapter Seven

It was hard to take in. When a massive situation first occurs the human psyche is programmed to deal with it. A rush of adrenalin prevents pain and keeps us going, but in no way are we programmed for the sudden ending of a situation.

The exhilaration Susan had tried suppressing in front of Jimmy felt trapped somewhere distant, like a voice beyond a wall of water. She half expected him to appear from around a door, leering at her with his wet tongue curling across his bottom lip as he had done so often. But he didn't. He was no more. Like smoke on a breeze he was gone.

There was just nothing except a vacuous silence that pressed upon Susan's loneliness, making her feel dead. He was nothing more than a ghost. Gone forever.

Her mind fuzzily thought of Mark. Tiny trickles of warmth began to seep back into her soul. Her Father. The trickles became streams. Her children. Great torrents of warm joy and love filled Susan's entire body. She felt alive again. Filled with the purpose that had kept her going over the last four days she re awakened.

She began to wriggle her wrists in the hope that she could break free from the restraints of the twine, but Jimmy had been careful to insure that she had no way of escaping, in no doubt as a means of keeping the police occupied for a little longer before they could follow him in her car.

She pulled and tugged but only succeeded in making her wrists burn as the twine rubbed against the tender flesh there. She gave up and relaxed a little despite her eagerness to run around and scream with joy at the regaining of her life. A life she honestly thought she could have lost at anytime over the last few days. She took a deep breath and let her body relax against the chair. She didn't care what happened now, it was over and she was okay.

A load banging sound suddenly filled the whole building. Someone was knocking on the front door and they were eager to get in.

"Help me! Help me please, I'm in the kitchen" Susan screamed as load as her dry throat would allow her.

Muffled voices consumed the air and Susan could hear several people all yelling commands and advice to people as they came around the house to the back of the house. She prayed someone would look through the kitchen window and see her.

Finally a solemn face appeared at the window. It was a male police officer, and the sight of him simultaneously thrilled and terrified Susan. She had half expected the police to be pleased to have found her but this man looked furiously angry and he didn't acknowledge Susan at all but merely yelled something which she couldn't make out to one of his comrades, before he disappeared out of view again.

Mere seconds passed before a huge gush of noise and bodies piled through the door.

Susan could hear voices shouting commands to her but she couldn't make out any one thing being said. She couldn't quite bring herself to feel scared after the last few days but she certainly felt confused and anxious.

"What's happening?" She finally found herself yelling through the din. "I'm tied here, what do you want me to do?"

The din didn't die down and she felt almost more alone than ever amidst this wave of people she couldn't understand.

Finally a hush began to descend and a woman police officer seemed to emerge out of the bodies with an air of authority.

"Are you Mrs Johnson?" She said with no manner of sympathy about her.

"Yes, yes I am Mrs Johnson" Susan tried again to wriggle out of the knotted twine, to no avail.

"Where are the rest of your family Mrs Johnson?"

Susan continued to struggle hoping someone would free her.

"I don't know. We were separated. I haven't seen them for days."

The Police officer signalled to one of her colleagues who came over to Susan and began to untie her.

"Mrs Johnson, if we release you from the chair, do you promise not to hurt any of us?"

Susan was confused

"Why would I hurt any of you?"

The WPC nodded at the man behind Susan and he finished untying the knots. Susan felt a cool sensation on her now stinging wrists. She brought them back around to her front. Around each wrist was a burnt graze from the ropes and the stinging sensation seemed to double at the sight of the raw skin.

"Mrs Johnson," The WPC began. "Where is Mr Bailey?"

Susan's heart sank slightly.

"You don't know?"

"No, we have people looking for him, but we could do with your help if you know where he is."

"He took my car. He drove off just before you got here. It's a Dark grey people carrier. There isn't much petrol in it, he can't get far."

The WPC put her hand on the radio that was at her shoulder and began relaying the information to someone. There seemed to be quite a flurry of activity outside, and before long Susan's hearing was filled with the sharp hum of sirens as some of the police cars sped away.

The WPC turned her attention back to Susan.

"Mrs Johnson, we are going to have to take a statement from you. We can do it here or back at the station"

Susan didn't want to leave. The thought of the outside world, a place where Jimmy still existed was scary. She wanted to remain here in the kitchen forever. Here was the last place she had seen everyone happy, and here was where she felt sure she would be reunited with the people she loved.

"I want to do it here, now!" The thought of her family made her feel sick, she longed to see them so much her bones hurt "Where are my family?" She asked terrified of any answer.

"Mrs Johnson, as of yet we don't know the whereabouts of the rest of your family, once we have ascertained that we can you will be the first person to know. Is it possible for me to send a couple of officers to search the building?"

Susan nodded as tears stung at her eyes.

"Thank you" The WPC nodded at the other people in the room and they set off. Susan had felt as though the burst of activity when these people had entered had involved a lot of bodies, but now when she looked there was only the WPC and three other officers. Once the two left top search the house the room suddenly felt quite empty again.

"My name is WPC Harrington, you may call me Beth. I work for the special branch of the police. I need you to tell me everything that has happened over the last few days, in as much detail as you can handle. I understand if you find it difficult, but the more you can tell us the better. Due to the nature of some evidence that is in our position, I have to tell you that at the moment we have to treat you like an accomplice. You have been harbouring a criminal in your home for almost a week and we have to take that very seriously. Now, I say again, for your benefit and mine, I need you to give me as much detail as you possibly can. Do you understand Mrs Johnson?"

Susan didn't understand. An accomplice? Evidence? Harbouring a criminal? She had been tied up, threatened and held hostage in her own home. Why would anyone do all of that the help a killer? She knew that trying to question Harrington would not have helped situations, and she just wanted to set things straight and set about living her life again.

"I suppose" She said in nothing more than a whisper.

Harrington ran through a full caution with Susan before letting her begin the statement.

She began by telling the officer about the meal. She even described what they were eating before Jimmy barged into the house, and knocked out Mark. She had almost forgotten how he looked lying there so fragile on the hall floor, but everything was coming back. Every feeling, every sight, every smell clear as if it was in front of her. She ran through everything until she felt violently sick and couldn't continue.

"Please, could I get myself a glass of water?"

Harrington gestured to her colleague who set about fetching Susan a drink. He placed it in her hands and she sipped it. The cold water gently pushed down the hot lump in her throat in cold waves.

"Please continue Mrs Johnson"

Susan took another sip and prepared herself to complete the arduous task ahead of her, but before she could the police officers who had been sent to search the house returned.

"Beth..." One said, nodding tilting his head to the side in a gesture for her to go and speak to them in private.

She did and Susan pricked her ears to hear what was being said, it was difficult as the officer was speaking very quietly, but the acoustics in the kitchen meant that she could hear every other word or so and piece together what was being said.

"Searched the premises... no Jimmy Bailey... family's... found... in living room"

Susan's heart leapt so high that it literally propelled her off the seat with joy.

"My family are here?" She yelled with joy. "Please. Please let me see them"

"I'm sorry" Said the officer "That isn't advisable at this time"

Susan's excitement began to transform into anger.

"What? Why?"

Harrington came over to Susan and placed a firm hand on her shoulder, pushing her down into her seat. But Susan didn't want to sit, and she locked her body.

"Mrs Johnson, you can't see them right now. Please, we need to continue with the statement. It's very important"

But Susan was not going to just sit two doors away from the only thing that had kept her sane for the last week. She had been through so much to keep them safe; she needed to hold them to make it all worthwhile. She needed to feel their warmth just to confirm that she was actually still alive.

"No, you don't understand. I need to see them" But Harrington didn't remove her forceful hand from Susan's shoulder, only raising the anger in the pit of her stomach and flaring it up until it was uncontrollable. Susan felt her cheeks heat up as though they were on fire and her vision blurred like heat waves were overwhelming her vision.

"I'm serious" She yelled "I can't sit about here, knowing they are a few steps away. Let me see them. Let me see them now!" She shook free of Harrington's grip. Suddenly she felt an exhilarating sensation. They couldn't stop her. This was her house and they were the police, they were supposed to be nice. They were supposed to help. They couldn't hurt her like Jimmy could have. "You can't stop me!" She barged walked through the officers, and barged them out of the way when they tried to stop her. She could hear them yelling for her to wait but nothing could have stopped her now, nothing in the world. She reaching the living room door and walked through with the biggest smile she had ever worn.

The smile slowly faded into obscurity. Susan couldn't quite take in the scene that lay in front of her. The smell that curled in her nostrils was rank and thick. It made her stomach turn and her eyes smart.

She scanned the room hoping that she was missing something, or that she was mistaken, but every inch of the room told her that she was not.

It was Mark that she saw first. He was lying in his stomach on the floor. He was the same as she had seen him last. The wound on his head was brown and rough from where the blood had dried and almost scabbed over. He looked just the same as she could remember. He looked just as if he was sleeping.

Then she saw her father. He was a contorted mess strewn across the sofa. If she hadn't known what he had been wearing that night she wouldn't have even been able to tell it was him. His clothes were bloody and torn, but nothing compared to his face. Above his eye was a bruised swelling so big that it made him look like his head would explode. There were open gashed across his face, sticky and brown with congealed blood. His arm was twisted behind his back at an unnatural angle that was impossible to achieve without dislocation.

The whole room was splattered with blood and the coffee table in the centre was badly damaged. In the corner of the table was a dark sticky mess with something white wedged into it. Susan could only assume it was her father's tooth, as his lip was badly slashed open and his lips were covered in blood.

Susan took this all in within a second before her joints went weak and she fell to her knees with a heavy jolt. She began to crawl over to her husband. She had no control over the tears that openly poured down her already sodden cheeks. She had no control over the guttural sobbing that issued from her lips.

"Mark!" She screamed in voice that was not her own. "Mark!" She reached him and held out her hand touch his face. "Mark, get up!" She cried. "He's gone now Mark, it's just me and you can stop pretending. He's gone!" Her quivering hand brushed against her husband's cheek. His flesh was cold and unusual. She knew he was dead but she couldn't let herself believe. She couldn't bear the thought of never speaking to him again or having him make her laugh. "Mark!" His name ripped at her throat as she screamed "Mark! No! I need you, please, I need you." She allowed herself to give in to a hopeless sobbing as she crawled in close to her husband's body and tried to embrace him. He was limp and cold and she couldn't hold him like she longed to. No matter how she tried she couldn't share an embrace with him. She felt so frustrated and empty. She just wanted to feel him close to her and never let go. She managed to cradle him in her lap. He head heavy in her arms and his body twisted and broken sprawled over her lap. She rocked gently, trying feebly to gain some comfort from the motion but feeling nothing but a sheer deep pit of empty longing.

She wanted to cradle her father too, but she couldn't stomach the sight of his poor bloody mutilated face.

She had trusted Jimmy. He had made her a fool. He had promised her that as long as she did everything he wanted, he would leave her family alone. When had he done this? When had he brutally murdered her family?

Harrington entered the room and stood at the mouth of the door. For the first time since the entered the house her face seemed to take on a little emotion, first discussed at the image that lay before her and then sympathy at Susan's obvious pain and anguish. She looked for a moment as if she was about to speak, but the words seemed to jam in her throat. She looked down and walked back through the door, leaving Susan to wallow in agony for a little longer.

Although she wasn't listening to what was being said in the hallway Susan couldn't help but hear the officers' conversation.

The woman spoke first.

"Well, I think we can safely assume that she wasn't harbouring Bailey through choice"

"How can you be sure?"

"Have you seen her? No one can lie like that! She didn't know that they were dead, Steve."

"We still have to question her and get all of the facts."

"I know my job Steve. Just leave her to grieve for a moment. She deserves to have a few minutes with her... family"

Family, the word echoed in Susan's brain. Family. This wasn't all of them. Where were her children!

She gave Mark one final deep hug. She didn't want to let go but she knew she could neither bring him back to be with her, nor stay like this forever. She kissed him on the forehead. His cold skin felt strange against her warm lips and tears pricked her eyes once more. Would she ever stop crying? She could barely remember the times when her eyes were always dry, it felt so long ago now.

Gently she lowered Mark's body to the floor and began to walk away, but she couldn't resist one final kiss. She lowered her face to his. He didn't smell the same as he had when he was alive. His lips were blue, dry and flaccid. She held her mouth to his and kissed him goodbye. It was the single most painful experience of her life and she could feel her soul leaving her body. At that moment she knew that no matter what happened in her life she would never feel truly happy again. She would never be able to let this go and she would always miss this man. He had been her life and now he was gone she was empty. The only thing left in the world was her children, but somewhere inside she knew that she was alone.

As pulled she herself away from her dead husband, eyes still closed, her lips stuck to his a little. She yearned for him to reach out and pull her back to him, to hold her to him and never let go. She felt it inside her so hard that she convinced herself it could almost happen, but when she opened her sodden eyes she could see nothing but the shell of the man she would always love.

She backed away, desperate to stay and try to somehow fix everything but knowing she had no power. No matter how hard she wished or prayed she would never see them laugh again, never see them or feel them or hear their voices.

With every effort her body could muster she turned away from the bodies of the two men that had made her who she was and walked through the door to where the police were standing.

The officers, who had been quietly chatting, looked up to her sheepishly.

Through a dry cracking throat Susan managed to speak.

"Where are my children?" She rasped

One of the officers who had been searching the house looked at Harrington; she nodded for him to tell her.

"They're upstairs, but they're in a bad way Mrs Johnson. You shouldn't go up until the ambulance has arrived"

Ambulance? Where they alive?

Susan couldn't listen to anything else. She darted up the stairs and headed first to Tom's room. If they were in a bad way they would need her.

She flung open the door of his bedroom so hard it almost rattled off its hinges as it smacked with a load bang against the wall, but they were not here. The room looked exactly as it had the week before, they were no here. They must still have been in Claire's room where Susan had seen them days before. Of course, why had she not checked there first? She dashed down the hall and pulled open Claire's door.

There they were her babies. They lay on the bed holding one another, like they had the day before. Susan didn't dare approach. The room smelled like the living room below and she couldn't bare it if she found that she didn't have them. They were her tiny little children and she had done everything Jimmy had asked her to protect them. If they were gone, she had suffered for nothing. She could have fought, or simply given up if she had nothing to live for.

Then, she saw Tom's eye move. It wasn't a huge movement and with the way her mind was running at the moment she couldn't be sure she had really seen it, but her heart was beginning to beat again.

"Tommy?" She gently called

His eye moved again.

"Tom!" Susan ran to her children, heart beating faster and hope filling her veins. She reached her son and pulled him up right.

His body was as limp and lifeless as Mark's

"Tommy!" She shook his slight body, but felt no resistance from his tiny limbs. But he had to be alive; she had seen him looking at her. She put her hand to his face and moved his fringe from his eyes. They were closed, but something was moving on them. Susan screamed.

"Get off of my baby! Get off!" She brushed away at her sons eyes, flicking a maggot onto the bed beside him. She brushed and brushed until all the foul little creatures had gone and then she screamed again because there was no other way to dissipate this awful feeling that pained her to her bones. She screamed and screamed as she held her son. She screamed until there was no sound left in her lungs and her tears ran dry. She pulled the cover back and saw her little girl lying as if asleep in her bed. She had been protecting her younger brother even in death.

She pulled Claire to her and held both her children tightly, tighter than she would have ever held them when they were alive for fear of hurting them. She clutched them as hard as she could and sobbed dryly into their corpses. She didn't think, and she could feel nothing but empty sickening agony. She didn't know that the police officers were watching her from the door until she heard the radio on Harrington's collar spring into life, causing her to jump and reawaken to reality.

They must have been gone when he brought her here. She had hugged him, and he had let her. She had felt some connection to him, and he had been tricking her. They were so cold. He must have killed them that first night. That was where he had been for so long he had viciously, soullessly destroyed them and lied to her. She would never have lied to people if she knew they were already dead. She would have had nothing to lose. She would have grabbed a knife and stabbed the bastard in the throat, had she known. She would have hit, kicked and punched him until he was as unrecognisable as her father. She would have had some vengeance and she would have had some chance at closure, or perhaps opportunity to save them, but she had genuinely believed they were safe.

He must have brought them up here and placed them together to trick her into obedience. He must have dragged their small bodies up the stairs and manipulated them into this position. What else had he done to them? She could not stand to think of it.

Everything she had done had been in order to keep them alive and all along here they lay lifeless.

She couldn't do this. She couldn't sit her cradling corpses and screaming. She would go insane, she was going insane. She could hardly breathe let alone function. What was she going to do? The only person left in the world that she had any connection to was the animal who had done this to her. She wanted answers. They had to catch him. She had to find out why he did this to her. She had to find out what he had done to her family. She wanted to kill the bastard. She wanted him to feel as much pain as her, and then she wanted him to suffer for the rest of his life.

The radio fuzzed again

"WPC Harrington, we have a stand of situation. He has stopped and got out of the car, but is refusing to come quietly. He's armed with an axe and has captured an officer. Negotiators at the scene are making no progress. Waiting instruction"

Harrington looked at Susan desperately clinging to her dead offspring.

"Shoot to kill"

Susan looked up.

"What? Can you do that?"

The radio fuzzed again and the police officer on the other end was about to speak but before he could a load bang echoed through the radio waves from miles away. Indistinguishable voices culminated into a fast hum.

Susan's mind buzzed. She felt nothing.

Was he dead? He would never know what pain he had inflicted. He would never suffer like this. She couldn't let out the breath trapped in her throat until she knew if he was alive or dead.

The radio fuzzed with a single voice. "Jimmy Bailey has been shot dead!"

After the shooting Harrington made Susan a very sweet cup of sugary tea and sat her in the kitchen away from the mayhem. She didn't ask her any questions and she didn't say a word she just sat with her hand resting delicately on Susan's.

The ambulance arrived soon after and Susan could hear footsteps rattling throughout her whole house. Crime scene investigators, paramedics and police swarmed about the place is a buzz of flurried activity as she sat here silently, eyes fixed to the floor trying to digest the world.

Rattling issued from the hallway and Susan looked up and towards the door. The paramedics were removing the bodies of her family. Four gurneys with what appeared to be long slim bin liners perched on top rolled out of the doors. She was overwhelmed by the urge to run over and stop the, taking them away from her. She knew that they were merely feted corpses now, but she didn't want to lose them even so. They were all she had left of the life that she had adored.

She didn't though. It took all her effort to restrain herself from throwing her body over them and refusing to let go, but she did, and then they were gone forever.

Harrington shifted awkwardly in the creaky kitchen chair. Susan knew it was time to say something. She opened her mouth but there was nothing to say.

Harrington sensed it was time to do something and took the initiative to speak.

"Mrs Johnson, do you have anywhere you want to go?"

Susan looked at the woman. She wasn't sure what she was supposed to say, but she thought about the question. She knew she had no friends left in the world, how could she explain all this to them. The police knew that she had not been harbouring a criminal, but the rest of the village had been scared and gossip travelled fast in the town. They would all, by now, be convinced that she had happily allowed her family to be slaughtered while she cavorted about with a murderer, and nothing would convince them all any differently.

As for family she had no one left. Not a soul in the world that she could confide in or ask for help. She didn't even have the luxury of all consuming hatred of Jimmy to get her through, he was gone too. Everyone in her life was dead. The closest thing she had to a friend now was this woman before her who she had met only hours ago and was only here because it was her job to be. She couldn't voice all of these things and simply shook her head.

"Do you want to stay here?"

Susan looked around her. Claire's size three wellingtons were still in the corner where she had flung them off that night. Her father's coat still dangled limply on the hook. Tom had left a sock poking out of his plimsolls in the shoe rack, and Mark had left his briefcase on the counter top, open and ready for work. There was a picture of them all alive and happy on a holiday in Cornwall last summer smiling through a clear plastic pocket. All of them brown from the sun and beaming out into the future, happy and together. They had been sat at a table in an Italian restaurant when a photographer offered to take it. Susan had been against it because it cost the £4.50, but Mark had insisted, and now she was glad that he had for this was the last photograph they had together. Again Susan could not convey this to Harrington and simply shook her head.

"Mrs Johnson, I can't even begin to pretend I know how you are feeling right now. And I have to be honest and say it isn't over. We still have procedures we have to follow and questions we need ask. We will have to justify shooting Mr Bailey and you will have to justify going into Chesterfield without telling a soul."

Susan looked into her eyes

"He told me he would kill them if I didn't"

Harrington's eyes developed sheen, but she swallowed down full tears.

"I know. I believe you. I will do everything in my power to..." but she couldn't continue. There was nothing she could do to make things better. "There are places you can go" She tried "We can arrange for you to stay somewhere, and with the circumstances we could arrange for you to start a new life somewhere fresh, for your safety"

"I don't want to start a new life. I was happy with the one I had"

Harrington looked a slightly frustrated

"Believe me Mrs Johnson, if I could get you that back I would. I can only imagine what a nightmare you have been through, and I swear I want to help, but there are routes that have to be followed, and we only have the ability to do so much."

Harrington stood up from the chair, took a step closer to Susan and crouched beside her so that they were face to face.

"Will you come to the station and finish your statement? I know it's hard but once it's done we can start moving forward."

Susan nodded

"We will find you accommodation in a hotel for tonight and then in the morning we will start looking for something more permanent. You don't have to make any decisions strait away, you can take all the time you need, and we will support that.

"I will arrange for you to speak to a councillor as soon as possible, I think you need to talk to someone who knows how to deal with these kind of things. Do you agree?"

Susan had no choice but to nod, despite already knowing exactly what she was going to do.

"Would you like me to send an officer to gather some of your belongings together?"

Susan shook her head. Harrington stood up, and Susan followed suit. She walked over to Marks suitcase, plucked the photograph from within and held it to her breast as she walked silently from the home she had loved and the family she had lost. She didn't turn to say farewell. She didn't notice Mrs Byron watching from her window, cigar hanging in her lips. She didn't hear the gossip, or the hushed whispers, nor did she see the neon flashing police lights and the officer who shot Jimmy, still splattered with the blood spots of his kill.

Chapter Eight

Beth Harrington began to awaken. She rolled over and pulled her boyfriend, Chris, close, until she could feel is warm naked skin against hers. He smelled musky, of night sweat, but pleasant in a strange way. Her alarm would be going off any moment, so she savoured these few sweet minutes before she would have to drag herself away from this simple pleasure that she looked forward to each night when she went to bed.

"Mmm" Chris hummed "Morning beautiful" He rolled over to face her. His breath was stale but she kissed him hungrily regardless. They moved closer together until she felt entirely enveloped by his tender muscles. She lived for this part of the day more than any other. This part and the moment she walked through the door after work to find him playing in his Xbox, but unfailingly besides a hot cup of tea for her.

"I love you" She vowed

"I love you too, babe"

Beth's phone alarm sprang into all singing all dancing life, almost vibrating itself off of the bedside cabinet as it chirped out their song.

"Do you have to go to work today, babe. It's Saturday. Why can't you get Saturday off every one in a while?"

Last night's horror flashed through Beth's vision. I can't today Chris. That poor woman, I'm not sure she will speak to anyone but me."

"I know, babe, but you had today off until last night, and you have been working double bloody shifts all this week to try and catch that wanker, now he's dead, you still don't get a break?"

Beth shook her head sadly. There was nothing more that she wanted than to stay here with Chris, especially after yesterday. It had made her think a lot. She hadn't been able to get it out of her head all night. Every day you have with the people you love has to be savoured. That sort of thing won't happen to everyone, no one deserves to lose everyone in one fell swoop. But everyone loses people they love every day. She wanted to delight in every single moment of bliss with those people while she could.

"Chris?"

Chris looked into her eyes. He was strong and looked it, but he had this face he pulled that made him look so vulnerable. He was doing it now, and he knew it made her weak

"Yes, babe"

"Do you still want me to quit and for us to start a family?"

Chris's eyes widened and his face lit up

"You know I do!"

"And do you think we can afford to do it?"

Chris was beaming.

"Well we won't be loaded, but I'm earning enough money to keep us comfortable"

Beth mulled it over for a final second.

"I guess I better type up my resignation before I go for my shift this morning then hadn't I?"

Chris grabbed her and squeezed her a little too light, but she didn't mind. She let him kiss her on the neck and then the mouth, she kissed him back.

The drive to work confirmed her resolution. She hated seeing all of the decaying misery of the world and being a police officer was the best way to get a bird's eye view. It was what she had always wanted to do and she would have been happy to have thought about a family with Chris before, but she had her sights set on being an inspector some day.

The drugs and debauchery in the world were one thing. You could clear it up and tell yourself that you were doing good things for the world, but this last week had shown her something else. A whole community had been too afraid to leave the house, and rightly so. She had heard little boys telling stories to one another of sleeping with knives under their pillows so that they wouldn't be got by Jimmy Bailey while they slept. She hadn't known the officer Bailey had killed. But she had seen him about. He had lay dying in a hospital bed for days, painfully bleeding to death, and nobody could do anything. It had scared Beth.

Then when she had gone into that house, well the filthy stink was enough to turn a rat away. And the sights. No one should have to see what Bailey had done to those poor people. The father had been mutilated beyond recognition. The corridor had said it looked as though he had put up a fight. The husband, they think he had bled out within minutes from the wound on his head. And those poor little kiddies, he had strangled them to death before placing them neatly together in that bed.

Susan's story was so sad. The investigators were convinced that she was telling the truth, and the locals who had seen her in Chesterfield explained she had seemed edgy and strange but they were too frenzied by their own fear to pay any real attention.

The way she had reacted at the sight of her family had made Beth want to cry out load and hold the poor woman close until the world seemed right again.

But she hadn't, she couldn't.

Beth pulled into the station car park and found her space. She stepped out, remembering the resignation in the glove compartment.

She pressed the automatic lock button on her car keys and headed into the station.

"Beth, isn't it your day off today" Shouted Mitchell, her friend, the desk sergeant.

"I've come in to see Mrs Johnson. Has she called yet this morning, I need to take her to the councillor at eleven"

Mitchell threw her a concerned look.

"Hasn't the boss man phoned you?"

Beth raised her eyebrow

"No, why?"

"He's in his office, I think you better chip on in and have a word with him yourself"

She frowned

"Fair enough, I had something to give him anyway"

She waved her resignation at Mitchell

"Chris finally persuaded you to let him make an honest woman of you?"

"Something like that Mitch, something like that"

Chapter Nine

The night before Susan hadn't left the station until the early hours of the morning. By the time they had arrived at the run down service station hotel the police had provided, it was getting light.

An officer escorted her up to her room and explained that they would have someone in the room next door at all times if she needed anything. All she had to do was ring through or knock and they would be at her beck and call. They explained she should try and get some sleep and then they left her.

Then they shut the door behind themselves as they left Susan stood in a strange place all alone.

She walked over to the bed. It looked lumpy and uncomfortable but that was of no consequence. She quietly, and without fuss, began to remove the duvet cover. Then, she systematically removed the bottom sheet from the patchily stained mattress, followed by the pillow cases, which she realised, were useless and cast them aside.

She then quickly scanned the room a task which she abandoned when she couldn't find what she wanted. She retired to the bathroom dragging the stark white impersonal bed clothes behind her.

She pulled herself up on the side of the bath so that she was standing on the ledge and could reach the curtain pole. She tentatively tested it with her weight, it was surprisingly sturdy.

She decided she did not require both sheet and duvet cover, weighed up her options and tossed the duvet cover to the floor. She felt around the parameters of the sheet until she found a weak spot and with a swift movement yanked it apart. She tore it right long the width, almost falling off the ledge of the bath with the motion. She stepped off the side of the bath and seated herself there instead. She felt a little way along the sheet again and ripped as before and then again until she had three strips. She knotted them all together and then began to plat. She had always loved to plat. As a child she would do it to her own hair, and then when Claire was old enough she would do it to hers. She felt almost content, not seeing the frayed strips of sheet, but instead seeing her daughters golden her and feeling it slide softly through her fingers.

After a while she had nothing left to plat. She stood up on the side of the bath again and looped the platted fabric over the curtain pole. She tied it tight and tugged it to check it was secure and when she was satisfied she looked away from her task for a moment and took a deep breath.

She felt in her pocket for a moment and pulled out the slowly crumpling photograph of her family. She looked at it for a while. Jack, her father, was wearing a white fedora he had purchased in a sea side shop to stop his balding head from burning in the sunshine. He bought a different one every holiday, and she had laughed at him and told him he looked like Hannibal Lector.

Mark had been wearing his Sex Pistols T-Shirt. She hated that thing! It had a tear on the collar that he refused to let her mend and a plethora of cigarette burns it had contracted from many nights of revelry he had spent wearing it. It was his favourite holiday shirt, and she had to let him wear it because he spent so much of his time confined to a suit.

Tom had been forced to have a haircut before they went. Susan had done it herself. He had squirmed so much that it was virtually impossible to cut it straight and he had ended up with it too short. Claire had laughed at him for days, and called him Forrest Gump. Susan had to admit she could see the resemblance, though she couldn't tell Claire that of course.

She remembered the night it was taken well. The meal had been delicious and they were all contentedly digesting it while chatting about what adventures they would get up to the next day. Jack was convincing his grandchildren they should go crab fishing in secret pirate coves and Mark and Susan were exchanging sly glances at the thought of a stealing away together for a day of passion and romance.

The photographer had been milling around nearby for ages but Susan's harsh look had kept him at bay, but once Mark had seen him there she had no chance of getting out of the holiday snap.

She had said that she would have given anything not to be sat like a lemon having some daft photo taken, but she hadn't meant it. Now she would give anything to be back there, to stay back there.

She held the photograph to her breast and clutched it tightly as she shed her final tears.

She looped the rope around her neck and jumped.

Involuntarily her muscles twitched for a while as her body let go of the life within. Finally after a few minutes, her body went limp, and the photograph of a happy time fluttered softly to the floor. Smiling faces of loved ones keeping watch over her until the police came.

End

Final Thanks

Barry Wood, Lorraine Wood, Ann Sellars, Phillip Lynam, Eldon Sellars, Nicholas Starr, Samuel Starr, My best friend (whom I don't deserve but treasure immensely) Siobhan Moore, My GCSE English teacher Mrs James who humoured and inspired me!

And finally last but not least... Sir Terry Pratchett for making me want to be half as talented as him and Rob Brydon for humouring a chubby kid (and her mother!) getting an autograph, by saying "just keep writing"

My Mamma Phyllis May Allen, who taught me how to string a yarn and is the best story teller in the whole world.

Printed in Great Britain
by Amazon